We All Need to Eat

We All Need to Eat

stories

Alex Leslie

BOOK*HUG 2018

FIRST EDITION

The production of this book was made possible through the generous assistance of the Canada Council for the Arts and the Ontario Arts Council. Book*hug also acknowledges the support of the Government of Canada through the Canada Book Fund and the Government of Ontario through the Ontario Book Publishing Tax Credit and the Ontario Book Fund.

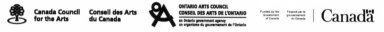

Book*hug acknowledges the land on which it operates. For thousands of years it has been the traditional land of the Huron-Wendat, the Seneca, and, most recently, the Mississaugas of the Credit River. Today, this meeting place is still the home to many Indigenous people from across Turtle Island, and we are grateful to have the opportunity to work on this land.

LIBRARY AND ARCHIVES CANADA CATALOGUING IN PUBLICATION

Leslie, Alex, author
    We all need to eat : stories / Alex Leslie. —First edition.

Issued in print and electronic formats.
ISBN 978-1-77166-419-6 (softcover)
ISBN 978-1-77166-420-2 (HTML)
ISBN 978-1-77166-421-9 (PDF)
ISBN 978-1-77166-422-6 (Kindle)

    I. Title.

PS8623.E845W43 2018   C813'.6   C2018-904121-8   C2018-904122-6

PRINTED IN CANADA

for Simone, still here

Contents

"love is form"

—Charles Olson, *The Maximus Poems*

The Initials

ON THE DAY OF THE INQUIRY, MY GRANDMOTHER stayed home in her apartment, drank red wine on her couch, watched back-to-back episodes of *The Passionate Eye* on CBC, and growled, "All those goddamn people are crooked anyhow," and then she ordered in Chinese food and fell asleep for centuries. At the inquiry the man running the show walked to the front and said that he had lost our book of names. My grandmother kept the list of names in the guest room, bottom left corner of the bookshelf. She opened the book and said, "This is my last birthday," and fell asleep again, while her apartment building rotated on the birdspine of a sundial. I went to the inquiry but never told her. She wouldn't have liked it. The man at the front said without memories there is no past and furthermore everything you need to know is on *The Passionate Eye* on CBC. I went back home, hands empty. There was no inquiry in the place where her mother was from because they burned the Jewish men on the beaches and the Jewish women were the smoke. "Do you know how to name children?" my grandmother said to me. "You take the initials of their dead relative and use them again and again so that the letters are never lost." This is written in a secret language. I often slept in her guest room except when I slept on the couch in the living room. I realized that the upholstery was patterned with her initials when I woke up to find her initials tattooed into my cheek. Alphabet welts, they faded but stayed. "Don't sleep on the couch," she said. "It'll make you achy all over and besides we don't get tattoos in this family." She showed me the magic trick to remove the core from an apple without moving any of her fingers. She opened her mouth and gold coins fell out. There was no inquiry and no report either because we all have new names now. We took our names from the book in the guest room or we wrote our names down in a guest book, we can't remember which, and there is no record of the threshold. When I got home from the inquiry, I lay down on my own bed and fell asleep. When I woke up, *The Passionate Eye* was on CBC again, part of a series she would have loved about Hillary Clinton and empowered female leaders. The next day we released her remains and the day after that it had been a whole year since her death. I received a book in the mail. All the rest had been sold or given away or disappeared. This book made it across the ocean, in the belly of a ship that my grandmother kept hidden in needlepoint art. A person with a jug. A boy squatting in shorts. There is no record of the boat's arrival. She always said she didn't know very much about what had happened, nothing that would be of much use anyway. An amnesiac with a stomach full of facts. I read the book but couldn't find my name, so I looked for my initials instead and suddenly they were everywhere, a survival of stars. I could remember every moment of the inquiry but nothing that had happened and no words that had been spoken. I'd sat in the front row and taken notes like I always do because it is important to have a record, but only the first letter of every word, all of the initials. There was no inquiry for my grandmother's relatives and the place they came from because she only used Yiddish to speak with her sister and with the dead. It isn't a secret but it isn't much of a history either. Only speak to yourself in a language only you can understand, and then you can put it away forever. The inquiry went on for a long time, until it was finished. No records were released until the '90s and photos taken by the Extraordinary Commission are blurry as images of interstellar travel or smoke as it leaves a mouth, so who can really tell. It went on for a while and I was the last one to speak and I forgot everything I wanted to know, and said, "I'm sorry, I have to go, I'm late for the ferry to the island to go see my grandmother." The lineup for the ferry was longer than it had ever been before. I waited for weeks and weeks, inching forward, past turnstile after turnstile, all the rows of cars winding around one another, so that I couldn't see where the line began or ended. Service had been horrible ever since the ferries went corporate. Finally I got to the front of the line, and a BC Ferries employee leaned across her desk and snapped at me, "Where ya goin? Duke Point or Departure Bay?" I said, "I'm looking for the boat with the book." She said, "It's Duke Point you want then," and gave me my ticket. It was very still. The parking lot stretched flat in all directions and I watched the people walk back and forth with their cups of Starbucks coffee and hot dogs in luminous foil wrappings. I watched a woman at the chain-link fence tell her dog to piss, command him like a soldier, kick at the mud in frustration. I watched a father tighten the yellow ropes over the top of his car to keep all his family's stuff strapped on tight so their camping gear wouldn't slide into the waves. I watched some children scream mindlessly, standing in a circle, small faces bright with cold. A bird fell out of the sky. I watched the ocean glow with its own secret light. Everybody rushed for their cars when the huge white metal boat appeared, the ramps attached to it like mechanical arms. Smoke drifted up off the water and got into our nostrils and eyes. Over the speakerphone system, the woman who'd sold me my ticket said, "There was no inquiry because she died before you learned how to write this poem," and I waited for the boat to start loading, scanned my iPhone newsfeed for updates, stared at all the unanswered messages from friends. When the boat was ready to load, the line of cars started to move forward. We were all going somewhere new. In the back of the car was everything I'd ever written in paper bags, the first letter of every word circled so I would remember how to read it even while sleeping. As long as the initials are stable, other things can move around as much as they want. My grandmother came walking off the ramp from the boat, holding a bottle of wine. She walked down the line of cars and everybody held their cups out the windows of their cars and she filled the cups one by one as she walked. She filled every cup less than halfway, so no one would drink too much while they were driving. She did not indulge and never touched the glass or the car with her fingers. She came to my window and I held out my cup and she filled it all the way to the brim without meeting my eyes and then the wine came pouring over the edges of the cup, red over my fingers, and she kept going down the line of cars. In the rear-view mirror, her body was very, very small. There was no inquiry because nobody knew where they were going or what was going to happen or how long it would take. It's a simple story. She vanished into the flat grey line of the parking lot's horizon, where the cement met the ocean in a blur, something solid becoming light. After she was gone, all the cars started to move again. I drove onto the ferry drinking from my wine glass. Like I always do, I went out onto the ferry deck and the salt wind sandblasted me clean.

The Person You Want to See

BODIES OPEN AND CLOSE ON THE MACHINES THAT FILL the weight room. A man drags steel from his chest—front push, cheeks taut, and the winged twin paths of his arms move to full extension. His chest under the surgical light. Mechanical bird, his slow flight. Then, release. Arms in, he folds back in, weights clink into a neat stack. He rises, breathes, heads to the water fountain in the corner. At intervals, everyone in the room goes to that fountain, bends down to accept its hook of water into their mouths. The gym is at the front of the community centre, its long glass wall facing the street. The thick rainfall casts the gym in aquarium intimacy. Cars whip past, their headlights the eyebeams of giant fish. Inside, bodies struggle in the tinted air.

Soma watches her body in the floor-to-ceiling mirror. Knee-length black shorts, a black T-shirt, broad shoulders. Behind her, women power the treadmills, knees and elbows in suspended animation. She is always the only woman on the weight machines. Men acknowledge her with nods. She knows them by the slogans on their giveaway T-shirts (*RUN FOR THE CURE 1998 Home Hardware CREW, Who are you RUNNING for*). Nobody speaks to her here, and that is part of why she continues to come back.

In the locker room, women peel clothes from their bodies. Steam is carried out of the showers on their shoulders and hips. A locker door bangs and shatters the warmth. Laughter of the exercise-bike women entering in a crowd. After the quiet of the office and her condo, the locker room is jarring for Soma, a thousand electric shocks to her eardrums. As she adjusts her bra, Soma notices the clusters of red specks on her shoulders. She checks the other shoulder. The same. Twists her head to inspect again. A pattern of delicate explosions, where the blood vessels submitted.

That night in bed, laptop nestled on her crossed knees, she googles: *blood vessels shoulders woman lifting weights.* The fitness pages instruct her to exhale while taking on more weight. Ease the speed of flow. Too much muscle development too fast and the body begins to break itself down, cell by cell. Gradual release of breath is easier on the blood. Trails leave her shoulders, head for her arms. She checks the rest of her body for implosions. Finds none. If she held her breath and lifted hard, how many marks could she make? Her body a map of ruined currents. She twists her torso, holds still for the MacBook camera's inbuilt eye to take a photo of one shoulder. She saves the image to the desktop.

When she double-clicks on the image of her shoulder, it springs up, huge, fills the screen. A planet in low light, a maroon edge, a dark world.

She googles weightlifters, selects Images. Men with skin-tight balloons defending their necks, shoulders, chests. Their surplus limbs; her faint red trails.

Soma has been coming to the gym every day for two months and she has felt the change. Not the slimming she expected, but a shift in texture. The ease of heaving the steel-and-glass doors to the government building where she works, doors that make the sound of a bank vault opening and closing. On mornings after she has lain in bed all night awake, the unexpected panic of being alone coming and going in surges, she climbs the stairs slowly and the secretary at the front desk nods sympathetically, knowingly. Her name is Phillipa and her son's wife passed away five years ago, so she makes a point of overidentifying with every loss in the office—deaths of pets, ailing parents, breakups. Phillipa left a card on Soma's desk when the news about Melanie got around. On the front of the card, a boy reached upward to catch a star, a Little Prince knock-off, a halo of text around his head that read, *You don't know what you're reaching for until you find it.* As if someone had died. Also? What an invasive bitch. But maybe Soma's getting bitter. Mostly she's just so tired, all the time. But when she feels her arms, they are hard and widening.

Soma's job at the passport office has rigidified as routine. She used to complain about it to Melanie—the endless supply of people who took bureaucracy *personally*, scream at her earnestly over the phone, *But my flight for Cuba is tomorrooooow*—but now she learns how routine is a crutch for numbness. Routine is everything to her now.

And today, the gift from Phillipa of a meditation book (left anonymously at her desk). Soma picks it up, makes sure to look down at it with a neutral expression—a careful performance for whoever is watching. She leaves the book on the magazine rack in the reception area with the Visa pamphlets after reading the first line on the back: *What you are experiencing is loss.*

Walking to her car, she texts her brother Josiah.

> *Generous anonymous coworker AKA*
> *Phillipa Lady of Perpetual Mourning*
> *left book informing me I am having*
> *a loss*

His response buzzes her hand as she slips her phone into her pocket. Josiah, now over thirty, texts like an irate teenager.

> *why r anonymous ppl*
> *all such fuckwits do*
> *they have meetings*
>
> *u need a new job*

Then,

> *ROBOOOOOTS!!!!!!*
> *!!!!!!!!!!!!!!!!!!!!!!!!!!!!!!!*

> *Yeah.*

> *u could move now*
> *why keep the condo*

big

> *Yes I am considering a year long cycle
> tour through the countryside.
> Thank you.*

haha fuck you too
☺

Fifteen minutes later, he texts:

> *what you are experien
> cing is losing*
>
> *loss*
>
> *sorry*

Soma has watched other people go through breakups on
Facebook. The suggestive status updates, half-scripts of a
melodrama, the sound of a palm clapping on a hard bright
screen. Sometimes a few old photos of the couple from
early days, posted ambiguously—these photos had a tendency to disappear. It was what people posted and quickly
deleted that was most self-revealing, Soma thought. People thought people didn't see, but that's what everybody
wanted—the satisfaction of watching life through a two-
way mirror. Then, eventually, the Rumi and Hafiz quotes
on letting go, the mourner giving public signs of personal
growth. The appropriate I-am-moving-on updates always
earned many heart icons (Soma hated these); any per-
sisting bitter or wounded posts were quietly ignored, or

condemned by receiving supportive comments only from the mourner's parents. *Things will look up love mom.* Soma has scrolled through many divorces. She read those stories distantly—the grinning avatars amassing sympathy. Facebook was not the place for tough love—you just looked like an asshole. *Have some self-respect,* she'd thought. This too shall pass. It was something buried deep inside her, this reticence. Really, this online gallery was only about who was watching you, not what you posted. Still, she couldn't stop scrolling.

When she starts to think about returning to Facebook, Soma isn't surprised to get unsolicited advice from Josiah. Over the past three months, he's called her up a few times a week from Halifax, making his two older kids warble pitchy hellos to Soma over the phone. In the summers during his undergrad in computer science he'd worked as a tree planter on Vancouver Island. Tree planting had transformed him, like finding a religion late in life. Soma dreads telling him about her weightlifting—doesn't want to weather his enthusiasm. An outlet, he will say. *I'm so glad you've found an outlet.* Like she's an electrical plug. These days Josiah works part-time from home as a graphic designer. In his spare time he makes prints of his photos of trees. He gave Soma and Melanie a triptych of wind-bent arbutus trees for their third anniversary—trunks entwined, sinewy, red and gold. His wife's father owns an American hotel chain. When they'd married, Soma sat in the first row, beamed politely, and thought, *You will never struggle.*

"Just post something," he tells her. "Then it's done with."

"What'll I do about the comments?"

"You just have to post something if you go back on. Otherwise it will be just—It'll be weird. Everybody knows you broke up. Melanie has like three thousand friends. You know?"

"What? What do you mean? Did she post something? What did she post?" Soma, who'd never been very into Facebook, had put an embargo on it since Melanie packed her things and left.

"Okay, okay. Never mind. Just give me your password. I'll do it."

His youngest, just four months, screams in the background, and the older ones sing, "PHONE HE'S ON THE PHONE QUIET QUIET QUIET HE'S ON THE PHONE PHONE PHONE," followed by maniacal pack laughter. Melanie had always said they all should live in the same city. She'd loved the kids, their insatiable love, how they shoved their fingers into her mouth, tried to unravel her tight curls. After their week-long visits, Soma always spent an evening on the couch, watching music videos or a movie on her laptop, slowly recharging. Melanie had laughed at her: *You're like an old lady.* Melanie, an only child, had lovingly followed and viciously mocked Josiah's novelistic Facebook albums of his family. Cherub-faced kid beside a potted rare kind of fern on his cedar deck. "Josiah is one step away from Gerber babies," she'd say solemnly. "You need to stop him."

"Won't I have to respond to what people say?" Soma says now.

"You don't have to log in if you don't want to."

But of course she would. She wouldn't be able to resist inputting her name and password, a jumble of the letters in Melanie's name and 0703, the anniversary of their first date, coffee and a documentary about penguin migration, which had made Melanie cry on the walk to Soma's car afterwards—"I can't believe how many of them *die*"—and Soma had kept walking, uncomfortable, thinking that she would not call Melanie again, that this woman was just too much for her, too much. So she hadn't answered the first two voicemails Melanie left after that date, both of them five times longer than any message a normal person would leave, Soma had thought, calmly, rationally, pressing Delete.

Username and password, muscle memory. *Raymorlo703*. She is a hacker's dream, these numbers embedded in all of her passwords. Banking, cell phone account, debit and credit PINs, passwords to dating websites she'd secretly cruised for the last few months of their six years together, not out of serious interest but for passive entertainment. *Lots of people must do this*, she'd thought. *It's innocent.* She'd aimlessly browsed the profiles of hopeful women, their open-ended self-descriptions and whimsical profile images. Rosie the Riveter; a panda holding a plate of brownies; a smirking Tina Fey. Half the profiles of people in their twenties used that actress from the TV vampire series Soma can't watch because of the blood—a wan, pastel cheekbone of a woman who isn't even very attractive, her vampire boyfriend cropped out. One woman wrote to her: *We have so much in common, it's like we're meant to be, can I see a photograph?* Soma had deleted the message in a panic, the sounds of Melanie showering after her ride home coming from the bathroom. Melanie had loved her cycle commute across two bridges and along the river. Now, driving those bridges, Soma looks straight ahead, the bike lane a hard margin against her memory. The yellow backs with silver stripes. Each one is Melanie.

"Why do I have to say anything?"

Her little brother is silent on the other end of the line.

"If you say nothing," he says finally, "you'll feel worse."

"God, we're all such"—she breathes the word heavily: "Robots."

"If spending time on that thing makes you feel like shit, just don't log in. It's a piece of shit anyway," he adds encouragingly. "Lots of people don't use it. It doesn't matter anyway," he lies.

She says goodbye and logs in.

The blue and white blocks, the faces in yearbook arrays. It's all suddenly so incredibly small, the quips and posts, tickets printed with script and hurled to the wind.

Click. Her profile. *Click.*

Her profile photo is a ferry deck shot taken by Melanie—gull origami nighttime flight, wind-slapped cheeks, Soma's hair exploded in a dark swarm. Her stomach twists at how post-coital the photo looks, as if they'd just fucked on the ferry deck against the Pacific-chilled white steel.

Melanie had bellowed over the rushing wind while taking the photo: "Put your arms out. Wider. Wider." Laughter. "Wider."

That smile, no idea what's coming. *You idiot.*

She deletes the photo, fingers popping wild across the keys. Heart absently hammering. Her drink slops onto her leg, just missing her keyboard. The smell of rum spreading down her thigh.

A powder-blue avatar pops up.

A no-her. Statuesque graphic. She can't even erase herself—there will always be another digital stand-in.

She scrolls through her newsfeed. Melanie's endless number of acquaintances, Soma's co-workers who she sees every day, Melanie's friends from veterinary school,

Melanie's friends from her bike-racing squad. A few friends from Soma's undergrad, from over a decade ago. But mostly these are Melanie's people. Profiles attached to her by the tentacles of her dead relationship. Where are *her* people?

Soma types into the blue-bordered status box, *Moving on is hard but*

Delete delete delete.

Well they say that

Delete.

The sun will come out tomorrow so smile smile smile

Delete.

Starting a new time in my life, looking forward to the next chapter.

Delete.

You are all going to die alone kids. HAHAHAHAHA!

Delete.

Settings.

Deactivate profile.

Are you sure you want to deactivate your profile?

And then the social networking system taunts her with loneliness, displays photos of her acquaintances, with a repeated message under each face:

Stacey will miss you,

David will miss you,

Leslie will miss you,

Max will miss you,

Matthew will miss you,

Janice will miss you,

Pat will miss you,

Ray will miss you.

Deactivate.
Click.

No one really watches the TVs in the gym—five flat-screens set on mute. Soma's weight routine (eight machines, then free weights) overlaps with the evening string of game shows.

The subtitles roll past:
[DO YOU WANT
TO TAKE THIS CHANCE
TO INCREASE YOUR
EARNINGS TO ONE
HUNDRED AND FIFTY
THOUSAND DOLLARS?]
The host's face twitches. The camera sweeps the audience.
[AUDIENCE APPLAUSE]
The contestant is in her mid-fifties. She perches in a black blazer with orange piping. She's wearing a taupe headband. *Who wears headbands?*
[WILL YOU TAKE
THIS CHANCE?]
[YES.]
The lights dim to a smoky blue, then dissolve into a white dome.
[SUSPENSEFUL
MUSIC]
[YOU HAVE REACHED
THE NEXT LEVEL
PAMELA.]

The woman spreading backward, legs out, blocky gums and teeth in a close-up.

[AUDIENCE
APPLAUSE]

Soma presses slightly upward. This week, she increased the weights to ninety pounds to see how it would feel. Her muscles climb and ache. The way her lungs feel when she spends slightly too long under water. She holds the weights there, in that place of almost too much.

[YOU'RE MOVING ON
TO THE NEXT LEVEL.
HOW DOES IT FEEL
PAMELA?]
[INCREDIBLE JUST
INCREDIBLE]

Soma can't catch her breath. Melanie loved these shows as much as Soma hated them. "I can't resist the pageantry," Melanie had said. "I love it for the same reason I love *Harry Potter*!" Soma would leave the room, stand in the kitchen, washing dishes until Melanie came into the kitchen and put her arms around her from behind, whispered into her neck, "Don't hate me because I love the things you hate." She said this about lots of things: Chicken McNuggets meals, documentaries about the British royal family, malls, dried seaweed, SPCA commercials, cargo shorts, long-distance biking. She used to go on daylong rides to Tsawwassen, the town by the ferry terminal, and come back and lie on the dog bed and moan. Soma never understood, watched her, mystified—this exuberant human with whom she happened to split life.

Soma holds the weights away from her body until the sensation shreds through her bared teeth. She could hold it here forever. She lets it back in. Slowly. Draws it back to her chest, lets it bear in hard, lets it press there. Back and ass rooted to the seat of the machine. Opens her legs wide. A feeling glows in her, a hand at the base of her spine. Melanie's voice in her ear: *Do you feel that? That's your pelvic floor.* A shudder tumbles through her.

In what bedroom, where had she said this? How many more times, these summonings in her body? Melanie's hand cupping the base of her spine.

She lets the weights go.

They slam down on either side of her ears.

She heaves, staring at the screens. Were there this many competition shows before the economy collapsed? Recession porn. The shows are far-ranging. High school math teachers performing Broadway musical numbers; B-list movie stars paired off and hacking out tangos; a show about a Christian family with twenty children, crewcuts and braids and checkered shirts. *Why are these people inflicting this on themselves?* Soma thinks. Melanie loved this crap. Especially the Christians, their colonies of offspring, their plans to renovate the double garage to raise more alpacas. *It's a family project! Everybody pitches in!* They are, Soma thinks spitefully, like a revivalist Chuck E. Cheese.

A girl, eleven or twelve, tells the talent show audience that she shares a bed with her single mother, that her father was an alcoholic who beat them. The judges prompt her performance of an old Etta James number.

[THE STAGE IS
YOURS.
IN YOUR OWN
SWEET TIME SWEET
HEART.]

The girl sings beautifully, body finishing with a bird's joy bow at a pool of water. Her face so open and pure, Soma has to look away.

She wants to tell them, *You don't owe anything to anybody.* She wants to tell them, *You can look away.*

It is easy to stop. This is what she has discovered.

Easy to stop answering email. Easy to come and go from the paperwork at the office, bring nothing and leave nothing behind. Move through the cream-and-steel lobby, the wax museum of co-workers. So easy to heave off all things. So easy. So easy to write back to Melanie's best friend, Jared, *Stop emailing me. I'm not Melanie and you never went out of your way to get to know me,* and delete his responding email without reading it. All things are contracts, not covenants. Easy to say nothing. Easy to stop acknowledging, and then reading, invitations. Easy to not move in relation to others. To amputate herself from gatherings. Melanie, who was a gathering.

The ultimate test of strength, the trainer had said at the introductory weightlifting class, is to be able to hold up your own weight. Hold yourself aloft. The trainer, a woman in her late fifties, made of thick rope and cantilevered joints, veins like exposed wires. Soma watched her, amazed. Melanie had been the one who exercised, duct-taped an uncle's caving headlamp to her bike before buying the proper gear. Her gear was always left piled by the front door for Soma to throw into the laundry room. Now when Soma opens their front door, she still smells Melanie's sharp sweat, almost reaches for her wet jacket.

The community centre's automated call for the weightlifting class had popped up on their landline voicemail a week after Melanie moved out. Soma hadn't known Melanie had signed up for a weightlifting class. She hadn't known Melanie had any interest in refining her cyclist body, her tendons already violin-tuned. *This message is for Melanie Lee Rhymer*, a voice had recited. *This is a reminder.*

Soma had gone to the class. She'd told herself it was to try something new, but really she had thought Melanie might be there. At the class, a woman in her seventies told them she was there for her osteoporosis. "Turns out my bones aren't what they used to be!" she said cheerfully, and the whole group burst into laughter.

The woman at the next locker looks over at Melanie. "Good workout?"

"Yeah."

"You were working hard in there."

It had never occurred to Soma that someone could be watching her. But, of course. What else would people do, while lying around grunting? "Thanks."

"How long've you been lifting?"

"Not too long. Couple months I guess."

"You're pretty solid."

"I think I'm getting there."

Small talk is a way to keep moving. Small talk is a kind of humming. Soma never understood this before—she always wondered at the uselessness of it. For her, cocktail parties and grocery store aisle conversations were exercises in failed lip-reading. Melanie had mocked this affectionately: "You just don't understand people at all, do you?" Now she understands.

"I'm George, by the way."

"George?"

"It's short for a name so horrible and ugly I refuse to inflict it on others."

"Georgephine?"

"Oh my god! Nobody's ever guessed before." Soma laughs, zipping up her jeans.

George's hair is shaved close. When she bends to untie and slip off her sneakers, Soma sees that the back of her head is surprisingly flat. *Like a zombie head*, Soma thinks to herself.

"I'm Melanie," Soma says.

George glances up. "Hi, Melanie. Long day?"

"Pretty average."

George nods at her shoes.

"Just a long day at work," Soma says. "Passport office."

"Sounds exciting."

"It is what it is." Soma shrugs and George nods. "The work is not letting people drive you nuts. And the dental coverage."

"I get that."

"Come for the living wage; stay for the free root canals."

"Well I'm a teacher. When we aren't on strike, we're arguing about going on strike. Good workout?"

"Amazing workout."

George strips quickly. A body that has lifted weights for years. She's probably in her mid-fifties. Something Soma's father told her once—you can tell someone's age by the backs of their hands.

"You're here all the time now, eh?"

"Pretty much every day," Soma says.

George nods, drifting toward the shower, pulling on her flip-flops. "It can get pretty addictive, once you get into it. Nothing better."

Soma drives home, hair damp from her shower, her shoulders and arms injected with honey endorphins. The cyclists pass her, brilliant fish in a parallel stream, their safety jackets smeared across her wet windshield.

At home, it takes an instant to reactivate her Facebook profile. The grid of friends' faces, her truncated history. And then, there is Melanie's face. She's shaved one side of her head, the hair on the other side scooped up around her ears and heaped boyishly, and there is another woman's face in the photo. Their eyes and cheekbones are matching and bright.

Don't click on her.

Don't do it.

Internet law.

What's on your mind? the status box asks her.

She types in: *The person you most want to see will become the person you least want to see.*

She presses Post and logs out.

She's getting stronger. A hinged thing. Flesh firm around her joints, her shoulders suddenly, one day, blades.

Soma has watched her body in the mirrored wall in the gym, watched her body change. Her neck plunges into her collarbone. When she turns and looks at her back in her bedroom mirror, it is a raised plateau. Her outside layer has peeled away. She remembers those anatomical models from high school biology class, human puzzles, their removable spleens.

The men at the gym now call her *bro*. One day, a shrug-nod, and then, coolly, *hey bro*. The luck of broad shoulders. Her new bro status pleases her in spite of herself. She moves the pin in the weights to 120 pounds. Mid-lift, she looks at her right arm, the new tough packet resting there. When she felt the new muscle for the first time, her mind flooded with worry: *A lump*. Her mind looks for reasons to panic everywhere. No, this is what she's been working for—this hardness. Beside her, a man strains on the piece of equipment dubbed the birthing machine. Weights attach to pads placed against the inside of each thigh. He squeezes and releases. *Aaaaahhhhhhhhhhhhhh*. Soma ties her shoelace to conceal her smirk.

The woman, possibly a dancer, who balances on the exercise bench every night. One arm extended. A weight at the end of her arm, muscle a perfect arc, a soft band. Soma watches. The pure control of motionlessness.

She logs in and the cursor flashes at her, asking her to fill in the box. *What's on your mind?* the pale-blue text taunts her, flashes, implores her.

She types in: *You are the only one pretending to be you.*

There are people and their ways of moving. There are the storks and the straight-necked and the sufferers, backs bent, ears blocked out by the steel orbiting rings. The men

THE PERSON YOU WANT TO SEE

who strut the length of the floor. The men who supervise the shapes of their muscles in the mirrored wall, sleeves summoned upright. How could anyone who goes to a gym think that women are the vain sex? Late at night, rows of men's hands wrap the metal bars. One man, compact and anguished, paces to the water fountain after every set of repetitions. Another guy guides his body through cycle after cycle on the leg press, extends and withdraws, pumping the bellows of a great machinery. Soma feels it occasionally as she lifts—a roughness in her blood. She has realized that her muscles have their own busy lives. Sometimes when she pulls on the weights, there is an absence there; sometimes, there is a humming, a throbbing, begun before she makes her demand. Soma ignores these quiet pulses, learns to pull with the same force every time.

When she tells Josiah about the weightlifting, she makes sure to slip it in casually at the tail end of one of their phone calls, but he stops and his voice lowers on the other end of the line. "Whoa whoa whoa, what?"

"Weightlifting," she says.

"That's awesome. How long? What?"

"Pretty much every day."

A long pause. "Since Melanie left?"

"Yeah, pretty much."

"Well, that's great, Lo, that's great, that's really great, good for you. I mean, I'm really glad you found an outlet." He pauses, waiting for her to say more, then pushes. "So, is it helping?"

"What's that supposed to mean?"

"I mean, you've been having a hard time. Dad called

me. He says you don't answer any of his emails or phone messages."

"That's because all of his emails and phone messages are about kale."

"Lo. Look. We all know what she did is pretty fucking terrible. I mean, who fucking—who just *leaves* like that? But, I mean, you two were always—"

"Always what?"

"Nothing, it's just—"

"Always what?"

His voice goes whiny, like it always does when he knows he's losing. But he can't stop. That's the thing about him; he just never knows when to stop. "Well you know as well as anyone. You two were always so different. She was just so much *louder*. You know?" Then he says the worst thing. "Maybe it's better this way." He breathes and says, "Anyway Dana says to come here for as long as you need, the kids want to see you and? They want to see you." He waits. "I want to see you. Do you see anybody?"

By the time she makes a pot of rooibos tea and checks her email, he's already sent her links to articles cautioning against daily weightlifting for women. *You just never know when to stop, do you, little brother?* She scans the cautionary paragraphs: not enough testosterone to build muscle as quickly as tissue breaks down, the websites inform her. She clicks on a link in a sidebar to an album of female body-builders; she scans for the dykes, scrolls through the stomach muscles and linebacker shoulders, sipping her cooled tea, the tears rivering down her cheeks. Everybody had known. Everybody had seen but her. And this is the part she cannot tell anyone, even Josiah—she does not understand why Melanie left, cannot explain it to anybody, how

Melanie raged at her that things had been off for a year and she'd had no idea, how could she have known nothing at all. She texts Josiah: *I feel so old.*

She's among the last ones there at night. This small group, buff stragglers. A staffer flickers the lights: library manners.

Soma blasts her body with scalding water in the showers, the steam pressing cloud formations against the walls, her knuckles tense. She checks her shoulders. A faint string of burst blood vessels again. Is this how it starts, she wonders, people who get into pain? Backslide, wander, trip into it. *No, I'm not like that. I'm not one of those people.* When she pulls the towel around her body, her skin is red. The burst blood vessels stand out in dark purple, a kitchen tattoo. She checks her right shoulder and, yes, there's the string of erupted blood vessels. Tonight, the damage reassures her.

In the locker room, the last women are half-naked, benches draped with yoga pants and rain jackets. While she dresses, Soma cannot help but inspect the other women's marks and scars. The tattoos. Soma would never get a tattoo. Too permanent. In undergrad, her roommate got a tattoo after she got a call from home that her childhood dog had been run over by a car. The tattoo was her dog's licence number, printed across the back of her neck. "You look like you have a barcode," Soma had told her, surprised when the other woman had burst into tears and rushed from the room, then for the rest of the term communicated with Soma only through Post-it notes. Melanie had leaned forward and whispered with a kind of awe, "Oh my god, I think that's the most insensitive thing I've actually ever heard. You're *amazing*." Soma had never been able to tell whether Melanie was making fun of her or praising her.

Both and more.

Long-term rented lockers are decorated with family photographs. Melanie would have made Soma rent a locker, stock it with protein bars. Her thoughtfulness could be controlling. "I'm kind of insidious," she had once told Soma proudly, and Soma had thought, *I want that.*

"Hey Melanie."

Soma looks up from unhooking her bra, shocked, to see George, her mild smile, and, startlingly, missing a tooth.

It's too late to correct her about the name. And, she realizes, she speaks to so few people these days that not being called by her own name isn't even really very surprising.

"Hello, Georgephine."

"Smoke?"

"Seriously?"

"Yeah. Seriously."

Outside the building, they lean against the brick wall.

"It's so *warm*," she says, and George laughs.

"You never smoked before?"

"Just not for a long time."

"Ah. I see."

"I've smoked."

"Sure you have." George smokes evenly, perfectly. "Anyway, look at you, the dedicated gym bunny, and I'm ruining your perfect health."

Soma smiles into the darkness. It's been a long time since anyone has flirted with her. "Gym bunny. Ha."

"Seems like you're here even more than I am."

"It's just recent."

"Is it? Lifting?"

"Yeah, and even the gym. I'd actually never been in a gym before."

"Really?" George's muscular body is a lean shadow in the dimness. "What made you go from zero to sixty?"

Soma hesitates. "Just a stupid breakup."

"Ah. Bad?"

"Yeah."

"Ah." George throws her cigarette at her foot, grinds it slowly. "Well then, that makes a lot of sense, Melanie."

"What?" Soma's neck snaps to the side. "What's that supposed to mean?"

"The way you lift. You know, like you've got something to prove."

Soma stares at George's profile but sees no hint of satisfaction—just her mouth set and calm, as if she's just read out the price of an item for sale. After a few minutes of silence, Soma realizes that George isn't going to say anything more. She leans back into the wall and watches traffic. Rain begins to fall, hooks at her lip.

The streets are dark, empty. Houses and houses and houses, stuffed with their hosts. The weights made tunnels in her. Dug her up again. She will go home again to the empty condo.

A white fish cruises along the side of the dark road. The bicycle drifts in its lane.

Soma swerves slightly.

The cyclist jerks, bends outward, pulled by the magnet in the centre of Soma's steering wheel.

She swerves gently again, hears the bellow of surprise

from the cyclist this time, how she can press herself gently into him.

She swerves again, comes back to centre.

His yell comes clear through the glass: "CRAZY FUCK-ING BITCH!"

This time she slows down as she swerves. Looks across the passenger seat and sees the cyclist's face. Not the hardened urban cyclist she'd expected but a teenaged boy clinging to the handlebars like a tree branch he's climbed too far out on. His fearful hunch, face angled across his neck, eyes stretched wide.

She swerves one more time and watches him go over into the ditch.

When she gets home, she huddles in her bed, the whole quilt around her body. Her body shivers so hard her knees knock against her chest. She pulls her laptop from the bedside table, opens it, and there's her Facebook page.

She types in: *your body was my home.* She presses Post. Sucks in her breath when she sees the words float there.

Hurriedly clicks her cursor in the blank space again.

Types in: *it isnt over if theres nothing left something was there then nothing*

Post. A tiny red 1 appears in the top right corner of her screen. She doesn't recognize the name of the person who liked her first post. Her body is still so cold.

Another blank space and she fills it in: *breaking open*
Another blank space.

She types: *nighttimes are worst when you sleep alone every night you feel alone all day you go back every time*

She types: *you planned it for so long and i had no idea. HOW.* Post.

She types: *this is so poignant are you watching?*

She types: *can a person actually just fall in love with a cipher?*

She types: *blood vessels break down very easily did you know I didnt.* Post.

She clicks the white camera icon to take a selfie. There she is, startlingly lean. Eyes large, the hard arch of one arm, the muscles visible. She clicks and the selfie stabilizes, unfocused and luminous.

A stranger gazes back at her from her new profile picture, jaw set, unmoving.

The image pops up beside each of the posts, a row of her, shrunken and staring, beside her words, the only true words she has spoken since Melanie left.

Sleep takes her down.

She prefers the gym late at night. The bodies and wheels. The low hum. The feeling of this day, and that day, and the next, and the next, entering and leaving her flesh. Her limbs pressed into rotations deepening their paths. Joints; grindstones. Her breath under one hundred pounds, two hundred pounds. The soft hammer against the front of her throat, marking out time. She is so strong now. Stronger than she has ever been. People rise and move from one machine to the next, busy with their private reasons for hardening.

Every day parts of her shift and tighten. Parts of her slacken. Soma presses herself until her bones bloom, her arms arc and make more room for more blood. There are gulfs and channels in her body, open spaces she has never known before. She enters them.

Stories Like Birds

SHE IS TOLD TO NEVER GO INTO THE OCEAN ALONE. OF course, she goes into the ocean alone.

Remote: they drove hours past a post office and then a tree covered in bras, nailed into the bark by loggers. Soma watched the D cups, stained by rain and the gold inner bark, flock past the windows. Nailed through, their savage steel nipples make her lightly finger her flat chest. She is twelve.

Don't go into the ocean alone, and she does.

The water yawns its black mouth wide, leaving a space to enter.

There is no hospital for hours, no phone reception: these are the reasons. This isn't swimming water. Open water, sweepings.

She goes in. There are no witnesses.

Feels the pull, her body throttled in a turbine, her salt-stung lungs, her body going deeper and deeper, beyond any decision.

The wave turns her; all that remains is the mute hold, inside the rotations.

Then she is spat out. The feeling that overcomes her, for the first time, the humiliation of the ocean's indifference.

No one has seen. The first thing she does is twist around,

beached, soaked and prone, the ocean withdrawn to a silver crawl below her drooping eyelid. Voices carry from behind the truck parked beyond the dunes.

The ocean's sound that a minute ago she was just one part of. Now she knows that it is made of tunnels.

When the friend throws himself from the bridge, this is what she knows: he was spared the sound of his own dying.

She walks slowly up the white beach. She hears her brother's voice, high and rubbed bright on the dunes, and she begins to run toward it.

When Soma is in her late thirties, she dates a woman with a four-year-old boy. The kid is terrified by the city's rapid-transit system, carves his fingers into Soma's palm, wraps one sneaker around the inside of her calf. This is the only time he claims her as his own. Soma doesn't drive and when she sometimes picks the kid up from kindergarten, she dreads these trips, blank-eyed commuters taking in the silent theatre, the kid grasping marks on the insides of her arms. The automated voice chants names of stations down the buried spine of Vancouver—*Marine Drive, King Edward, Broadway City Centre*—and the numbness enters her blood-stream at the place he is anchored.

One night in her girlfriend's apartment, Soma clicks a video on a work acquaintance's Facebook page and plays it once, twice, and the kid, always watchful of her, runs over, demanding, "What's that! I want to see!" The video shows a flock of birds travelling above a lake. The birds move in a sheet, spreading and folding, a surge of interlocking triangles that tents the lake, opens a slow, flurried eyelid over the furious blue, the sky. The kid stares at the video, transfixed, his fingers on Soma's neck. He has his mother's habit of lightly touching the person he is talking to. They are both nervous, tactile.

"Again. Again. Again," he chants.

The video solves Soma's problem with the kid's fear of rapid transit. When he begins to clench, she announces, "Birds!" and he repeats with anticipation, leaning into her, "Birds birds birds." Passengers watch, a few always peering at the screen to see what the kid responds to instantly, his head flopped to one side, his smile spreading. She doesn't know why the video works: she accepts its magic and repeats it endlessly. The kid's eyes tunnel into the morph and sway of the bird cyclone. Hypnotized, he nods when she whispers, "Again?"

They get through the video six or seven times before their stop near the girlfriend's apartment. She always puts the phone on mute because the soundtrack is the filmmaker (in a boat in the centre of the lake, she assumes) bellowing, "Oh my god! Oh my god, here they come again!" and she knows that the voice, its mock alarm and adult lack of awe, will turn the kid off. The internet is full of videos intended to transfix you, Soma knows; everyone has a little digital spell to fall back on. Reluctantly, she comes to love the small warm stone of his head on her shoulder, the whirling silence of the video, how completely she can fulfill his request.

"Birds, birds."

When the kid's mother breaks up with her, Soma sits on her bed in her apartment, slips her phone out of her pocket to text a friend. Instead her thumb pilots itself to the internet icon. Then to the window with the bird video, always kept there for the kid. She presses the Play button.

The birds fill her hand. The sound from her throat falls into the black-and-blue core of their endless turning. Her hand is full of shifting wings.

It is the video she watches when she loses her job to government cuts the following year; when her oldest friend dies six years later in a car accident. The video is bookmarked between a news site and an online dating service she never checks and never stops paying for. She never shows the video to anyone else. She wonders how the kid survived without it after his mother asked her to disappear, and how she responded to his requests for birds.

Soma is seven years old the first time she leaves home. She is seven and she is leaving. Later, much later, leaving will reveal itself as always more work than staying, but when she is eight and nine and ten and eleven, leaving is effortless, a matter of launching—whatever comes next is irrelevant.

She is running from the rage in the house where she has grown up. Running down a hill, past cherry blossom trees in a row like cheering people, pink cloudy heads of blooms all the way down, and she is travelling down a very steep hill and oversteps, and for a moment there is no ground, the angle of the hill deepens, her eyesight bows down to the sky and she's sure she is about to slam into the dappled pavement, the even squares laid down by the city with the date stamped at the end of every block. And her whole face will scrape off and require surgery that will leave her looking like a tire tread forever. But her back saves her, it whips up, and her knees are in front of her instead of her feet. She falls backward—falls vertically onto the hill made flat by the impossible thrust of her body, her shoulders pressed toward each other, her hair damp with sweat and blood and the bright pain of light through the cumulous cherry blossoms. This is how far she gets the first time she leaves home.

Her scalp is soft in one place. She sees billowing fluorescent clouds for weeks. Nobody believes her except for her brother when she whispers to him, "I died." He looks impressed, asks her what it was like.

Her concussion is not a concussion: it is a confirmation. She ran away and it was just a mistake that she returned, a snafu on the road to her ultimate exit. She will go.

At night she shuts her eyes and sees blowing streets of white light, sees her grandfather who died the year before. Leaving doesn't happen all at once, but in pieces. It begins with running. Her brother nods fearfully when, once a day for a month, she tells him, "I died." She relishes how in awe he is. He asks her what it was like, again, again, and she shakes her head at the pinky finger he holds out to guarantee secrecy. She shuts her eyes and remembers the footless step, her celestial headache blooming from the eyes in the trees, the people living everywhere in the air. She bargains with him to rub her temples in gentle hoops in exchange for news of death. Then she denies him, smugly.

She knows she can't describe it to him anyway. The impassive thundering in her body, how it holds her down. How she returned to earth with the understanding that it was temporary.

She and her brother will sit across from each other in a restaurant in their twenties, after the friend's death, each one older than the other, ages as interchangeable as their water glasses, and confess that they were both always afraid living in that house and both swallow sound and still leave their bodies on a regular basis. Both will have had lovers who argue with them, try to convince them to stay. Her brother will tell her that he's marrying his girlfriend, his rich WASP girlfriend, daughter of a hotel-chain owner, because she's pregnant.

He will say to her, I think I can do things better.

She will respond: People are people are people.

He will say to her, I wish I remembered more, and she will say nothing.

She will remember his face when she told him she knew how it felt to die, how expectant he looked, how excited, how she was the one going further and bringing back news of the future.

There is a spot on Soma's head where the flesh is still soft even now, will always be an entrance to defend, an indentation that she rests her palm against when she gets too tired. She places her hand on that patch as if in prayer, leaning into her elbow, watching the sunlight slip at an angle through the splayed fingers of the world. She watches the video again and again and misses the boy she grew up with and her head rings in this one place.

When she's halfway through her twenties, a friend from her undergrad degree jumps from the highest bridge downtown. A day after the hysterical phone calls from the friend's father, comes a message from an undergrad acquaintance sent to forty-seven mutual friends on social media. She focuses on the flawless black print on the screen, the elements of print becoming small hard-edged men, the permanent bellies of *d*'s and the outstretched wings of *T*'s, the perfect straight tunnels of *O*'s. The screen has strobe depth; the blank spaces between the incisions of symbols, bubbles. She scrolls down the responses, a few *OMG*s. One person has written *!!!!!!!!!!!!!!!!!!!!!* followed by a jumbled string of emoticons—faces of animals, tiny houses, stars and knives and forks.

Punctuation has the advantage of being an end in itself, a pure digital howl.

She is at her desk at her transient job at a gallery, and someone is asking her how the new coffee maker could have broken down so quickly. The coffee machine is important, and Soma startles herself by turning and snapping, "There's a Starbucks on every *fucking* corner." Her feet are so hot inside her sandals, as if she's standing balanced on the bright scalp of a light bulb.

She copies the message into an email, types, *what the fuck*, and sends the email to an old friend who knew the dead friend for as long as her. She spends half an hour sending messages to which she does not expect responses.

Every day, she crosses two bridges to get to this job. This city of bridges where she was born has always known jumpers. They are a routine fable, unseen and accepted and rarely mentioned. She searches the city on Google Maps and examines the blue and black lines, the warp of inlet and coast and crossings. The message about her dead friend still open on her desktop. She thinks, *This city is just a set-up, look at all those bridges.* She's old enough to recognize when she's at her most dramatic, her most paranoid; these extreme thoughts have become another thing she has invented in order to outsmart. Still, she tells herself, people jump from buildings as often as they jump from bridges. It is only a matter of levels.

She googles the height from which a human body must fall in order to die on impact.

And is this different for water and pavement?

And does water become solid if a body approaches it fast enough?

And before impact, has the person changed into something else? An angel, a stone?

Stop.

"Have you wanted to kill yourself?" Soma's oldest friend, who was close to the jumper, asks her.

They lift handmade noodles from bowls in a Japanese restaurant across from the downtown public library. The friend's eyes are hooped in navy, which she has tried to conceal with makeup, producing an owl's regal, remote stare.

Soma swallows, adds, "I've wanted to, a few times."

"Who hasn't?" the friend says.

They eat.

The jumper has flung himself into the new gulfs opened between the people who knew him. He did not leave a note. This is a thing people who did not know him ask Soma—did he leave a letter? It is a thing people know how to ask.

TV trained them to want a body, an investigation, a discovery.

Instead Soma googles *are bodies found when people jump from bridges* and the name of her hometown and reads that in these incidents the body is almost never recovered. She googles *tidal patterns*. Eyes the charts, the long loops and the filigreed eddies. Absurd that the city exists in the midst of all that oceanic confusion. A city is a simple thing, an afterthought, an aspirational sandhill.

His body is not breaking down, is not being deboned by currents and all the salts of this world and the one under it. His body is rotating, hand to heel, pinwheeling through open space. She remembers him waving across a room at a fundraiser, making small talk at a housewarming. These moments lack staying power.

What remains: an endless, gentle tumbling, all parts of him intact, punchlines and organs. For months following his death, clothed and orbital.

She cannot imagine the moment he jumped—he was a shy person like her, never forthcoming, arrested by neuroses—but she cannot stop his somersaults. His loose, beautiful sandy hair, perpetual motion. He is the first person her own age who has ever died.

Soma rides her bike around her family's neighbourhood late into her teenaged nights, years after her mother left. Her mother who visited sporadically but never stayed, though her father promised for years. Told legends that became beautiful with disappointment. Under Soma, the bike is light, another mechanical component of the agile darkness. She rides for hours, her legs slackening with exhaustion, her pendulum knees swinging, because this is her only time alone, inside a world of distant graffiti branches and faceless houses.

The habit becomes convenient during her first relationship, a girl from her high school who lives in a neighbourhood down the steep hill. Soma leaves and returns during the night, glad that she gets to leave, escape on the cold metal speed of her bike, glide off down the fast black streets, hop the boulevards sideways, tease the gutters with the stripping rims of her wheels, still feeling what she had done inside of her, the wide warmth of that, but travelling fast away from herself, like a pellet of blood that whips up and down all the wet speedy roads of veins but never makes its way to its source.

She rides until she is tired enough to return. She crawls tired and drained into the heat of her bed.

There is the fall down the bike's glimmering chain before the hill assumes its shape, the city flattens into a bowl, darkness flanked by ocean. She stays out on her bike for as long as possible, the ache entering her calves, settling in her feet, exhaustion that does not burn out but hardens in pockets.

She continues until she has to return to her house, her body spent enough to crumble. Immediately, she sleeps.

Her brother, always younger no matter how much time passes, never the escape artist she learns to be, complains to her that their mother turned up and screamed deliriously at their father for hours, then left and returned, left and returned, each time louder, the tide coming in, until she leaves for good.

One night when she was eight or so, her mother entered a new kind of rage like she'd never seen. Plates jumped and danced across the floor. Circles of light roamed the ceiling. A spoon carved a ringing silver halo around her mind. Her brother was a whisper in the collar of her shirt, then gone. Soma ran from the house and felt her mother's thunder pursuing her. She outran herself.

The park at the bottom of the street was full of pockets of translucent shadow and soaked grass. Children didn't come here at night. She had been told not to go to the park alone at night and she did. Clipped trees like great hot air balloons unmoored in the black. Inside one of them, a round dusty room, gnarled branches, reaching upwards, holding the roof up. Soma crawled in, curled up on the dirt and slept. Dreamed about running, a chain of flipped hills.

She was awakened in early morning by four raccoons watching her, bored, from the entrance to her human burrow.

She staggered to her feet, pushed the dirt from her jeans, and wandered up the hill back to the house she was from.

The last summer, Soma remembers—the downward pull of the hill, her brother's blame pulling her back to the surface, and the girl she fucked to learn how, how she rode her bike until dawn more than once, light rising through her eyes, a dawn in her blood, her arms and thighs crossing each other's revolutions, the soaked streets rivering and the door shutting again behind her, body throbbing mutely past decision, how her brother said, furious at her door frame, "You're never around anymore," how she responded, tired of the weight of their savagery.

"Don't worry, I'm already gone."

The Sandwich Artist

MY FATHER ALWAYS TOLD ME, "IF ANYTHING TERRIBLE happens, treat yourself to a nice meal." Advice passed on from one generation to another, a recipe for a history of starvation, but I didn't know that yet. I only knew Chinese five spice BBQ pork with pineapple and red glaze, fish and chips bundled in greasy newspaper, corned beef boiled in bags, rotisserie chickens leaking orange condensed steam over tinfoil. I knew sweet and sauced and salty and, later on, spiked. I knew broiled and fat 'n' happy. I knew how to drink a bad day out of a gravy boat. It isn't that I'll run out, it's that in the beginning there was never enough.

When my brother hadn't left the house for three weeks, my father called me up and said, "Hey, I bought a Heritage Farms chicken, want to come over?"

"How's Josiah?"

"We'll need a lot of garlic, right?"

"A lemon," I said. "Is he any better?"

"Yeah, he seems better. What else."

"Rosemary."

"Dried."

"I'll bring some from my pots."

"Bring extra so I'll have some in the fridge. I have wine," he said.

"Fresh garlic."

My father never bought fresh spices, just endlessly replenished the giant containers of powdered garlic, onion, and oregano from the bulk bin at Real Canadian Superstore. The containers lined the top of the family stove, unmoving as gravestones. The garlic was the texture of instant milk and smelled like chicken soup mix. Its scent flavoured my childhood memories of camping trips, burgers laced with its rank tang. When I started to cook for us, after my mother left, I walked to the grocery stores and asked a white-aproned man restacking the peaches where I could find the garlic. "I don't know what it looks like," I told him. He looked at me like I was playing a prank. At home, I scraped at the sheer white outer tissue, then sliced the whole bulb down the middle and hacked bits out with the point of a steak knife, flung the massacred pulp into the pan, juice stinging my eyes. Now, my fingers dismantle garlic instinctively. I press a knife's blunt side to a clove with the flat of my palm to loosen the casing, and the smooth white clove falls free, its side fingernail-smooth.

"My garlic not good enough for you?" he growls.

"We need lots of olive oil for the skin. You got enough?"

He's always running out of something.

"I have lots of oil, just bought a new can." I wince. He buys his olive oil in bulk too, in a giant can with spout, like an emergency gasoline supply.

"Tell Josiah I'm coming."

"He knows."

My roast chicken is perfect. If you know how to make one thing perfectly, you will always get invited back. It's your basic French roast chicken. Remove the neck from the cavity, keep it for the *jus*. Halved lemons and salt and crushed peppercorns and a few garlic cloves fisted into the belly, stretch the skin over the neck hole, pin it in place with a skewer. Massage the chicken with oil, coat the skin with rock salt and cracked pepper. Not table salt; the flavour is french-fry sharp. Use salt with enough substance to cook in the oil. Yogourt makes the skin brown and thick, but I prefer the crunch of oil, salt, pepper. Bacon fat if you want smoke. 375 oven until it browns, then 350 with a tent of oil over it. Thirty minutes to the pound.

Baste often.

Forget everything you've heard about latchkey kids. I loved the freedom. The unclocked arrivals, my backpack's contents spread out across the three couches, the TV guiding me into the trashiest dead ends of adulthood. I microwaved bags of frozen gyoza, dressed them in Kikkoman teriyaki sauce and honey, and watched drag queens claw each other's gender identities on *Montel*, watched Judge Judy preside over trailer-park divorces, watched Maury Povich call paternity test results like a hockey referee bracing for a fistfight. Hustlers and salesmen populated my afternoons while I spooned up Bear Claw ice cream, sucking frozen marshmallow bulges from my spoon while middle-aged women bemoaned their sex drives. *It doesn't even work in the bathtub anymore.*

But my favourite show was *Boot Camp*. Obese teenagers with multiple misdemeanours scoured toilets with toothbrushes and did push-ups while men in security uniforms bellowed down at the folding adolescent bodies. Sally Jessy Raphael, my favourite TV personality for her inexplicable cruelty and rhinestoned disdain, presided. In my memory she's a redhead in a white suit with a gaudy red collar. Cruelly cut rhinestones. The teenagers sob, then are blessed by her hand. She absolves us, her watchful monsters.

I watched, inhaling my Ichiban instant noodles with an egg swirled in, my hot chocolate bloated with marshmallows, Kraft Dinner with butter and instant milk crystals sprinkled on like Pop Rocks. I felt sorry for the kids on the screen, my fellow prisoners who'd somehow had the bad luck of getting caught. But I disapproved of their weakness, looked down on them for losing it on camera. How they sobbed and pleaded for release—*I will get better, I will be better.* I watched, the judicious observer, stuffing myself like a beast being prepared for her roasting day. My hunger was insatiable.

After my mother left, my father put Josiah in after-school care; he never asked me if I would prefer to go too. I was a small adult from now here on in—our secret bargain. Until my father brought Josiah home on his way back after his work commute, at sevenish, I was alone. Those hours, after Rosie O'Donnell and Montel and Judge Judy, were when I learned to cook. My father started giving me weekly cash in envelopes. I pushed the shopping cart from the store. Five blocks to our house, neighbours accustomed to my routine, the clatter of the cart on the dimpled sidewalk. I white-knuckled it, always afraid that someone would pursue me from the store for taking the cart. Nobody ever did. My fear placed its wide hands on my shoulders and pushed me forward. But who's going to chase a ten- or eleven-year old pushing a cart full of chicken breasts, garlic and spa-ghetti? I ferried my ingredients up the hill.

I loved frying the most—*sautéeing*, the cookbooks I started to check out of the library taught me. A new vocab-ulary of taste and heat.

I was twelve, thirteen, fourteen; I melted olive oil and butter together, swivelled the pan until they rose in a brown lather, lay the chicken breasts skin-down, inhaled the crackle. I seasoned my meat well. When they got home, it was always seasoned and ready.

My father catches me at the front door before I can head to Josiah's room.

"Josiah's tired. So maybe we'll just cook for a while, till he has time to come around."

I hear the dim snarl of Josiah's electronica from his room at the back of the house. He's almost twenty, not a baby anymore, but he's our baby.

My father studies my face. He's going to tell me what's going on with Josiah. Why he won't return my calls, my emails, Facebook posts that linger on his wall. "Soma," he says. "I remembered to leave the chicken out to let it come to room temperature. Like you said."

I nod. I've lectured him countless times. *Never cook chilled meat, it makes it tough.*

"Did you dry it before you oiled it?" I ask.

"Yep." If I haven't been able to make my family happy, I've at least taught them something about how to eat.

We set to work on the chicken. He hasn't preheated the oven. "I forgot what temperature," he complains, "because you never write anything down."

I oil the skin, drop the neck in a saucepan of water to simmer for the jus, plunge my hand wrist-deep into the bird, fill it with lemons and garlic and a small hoop of rosemary. Cold in there, small ribbed cave. I pull and seal the skin over the hole. I snow the bird with salt. Always hold your hand at a height, so the salt distributes evenly.

"Aaaaaaaaah, looks great."

He slides the chicken into the oven. The door shuts gently. He bought a new fridge and stove last year. The springs are still eager, jump shut. The stove he threw out was the stove of my childhood education, those adolescent banquets prepared in afternoon isolation. The light in the oven was shot for half a decade. Two of the burners were crooked from use—my hands and wrists developed to rotate the slanted pans so the meat cooked evenly. He didn't tell me when he threw out the old stove—I arrived one day to the new one, its face gleaming mutely. It felt like my first car had been stolen. I didn't know that I had loved it, the chipped silver-faced dials and the top encrusted with a generation of spitting pots and my father's granulated garlic, my first serious burn inflicted by steam, not sunlight. How years of family flavour become paint.

He flips the oven light on and we kneel side by side, stare in at the bird, pale and naked above the glowing bars.

"Glad you're here," he says, puts an arm across my shoulders.

Josiah has locked his bedroom door. I pound on it, a Sally Jessy Raphael warden all over again.

"What the fuck. I can't believe you. I came here to see *you*."

I haven't come in a month from my bachelor apartment on the other side of the city—I've been swamped in shifts at the restaurant where I worked as a line cook, the most recent in my string of shitty jobs. Josiah works out of his bedroom, programming online games that people buy from a friend's site. He has online friends he's worked with for years who he's never met; last year he drove across the border to meet a few of them for burgers and nobody got along in person, so they went back to being techie internet soulmates. He emailed me the master password a year ago and I trolled his games, searching for a way into him. A world of elves, trolls, and fairies. Rapunzel-like plots. Rescues and escapes. I surfed through, knowing he would look up my catalogue of movements indexed to the username. The next time I saw him he was eager and bashful. "I liked it," I told him. "A lot of the games seemed to be about love." He shrugged, gave me a disappointed look. "All games are about love," he said.

I pound the door again.

His voice thuds through the hollow-core wood. "Go. The. Fuck. Away. Now."

Cranks his music up, a remix of songs I don't know.

He's the person I have most memories of feeding. His birthday cakes, his favourite potatoes, the instant Farkay brand Chinese noodles I tossed in smooth peanut butter and honey for him until his voice broke and his legs swept out from under him, the slender trunks of poplars. He was so eager, so easy to fill.

We were never siblings who gave gifts. People mistook our silence for distance. Friends didn't mention our absent mother—thought it taboo or rude. But I was frequently told by other people's mothers, to compensate, *You're*

61

lucky to have such a great dad. As if one thing can replace another. Josiah and I knew better, and because we always already knew, we didn't need to say it.

Nobody had spoon-fed us. We were greedy but self-sufficient. Hard with want. When I was about fourteen, my father started going away on business trips for two days, three days. Longer and longer. Another kid's mother dropped Josiah off from his after-school daycare. I bought us Ruffles, Cheezies, cheddar Bavarian smokies, bacon, tubs of frozen cookie dough that we ate raw with spoons from the bucket. Food we never ate in front of other people's mothers. I rented the old Disney family movies. *Candleshoe, Escape to Witch Mountain.* Boxes of frozen mini sausage rolls. We were a trashy cocktail party. Mini quiches. Root-beer floats clanked together. We slept on the thick dirty carpet in front of the TV. Bellies painfully hard, pressed together. Conspiracies of sugar and loneliness. We ate and we ate and we ate and we ate and it was never enough.

I was around sixteen when I got my first job. I considered myself as an expert cook, a home chef, and assumed it would be easy to get a job as a "line cook" (a term I picked up quickly on Craigslist). I fantasized about telling friends casually that I was a sous chef. I didn't consider any other kind of job. Kids from school worked shelving books at the public library, coaching kids at weekend soccer camps, tutoring third-graders in English as a second language, but I had to cook. Writing a resumé for the first time was a humiliating process—under Qualifications I put "knowledgeable about foreign cuisines," deleted that, and replaced it with "well-read in world cookery." It didn't occur to me that I would need basic training in food hygiene or technique. I already knew everything I needed to know. I dropped my one-page resumé off at local restaurants and waited, spending my afternoons watching the same talk shows I'd always watched, but now I glared at the adult participants with impatient contempt. Why didn't any of them have jobs? I was suddenly intent on everyone in the world pulling their own weight. It was clearly the only solution. What did they do all day?

After a month of job searching, nobody had called back. Subway left a stack of leaflets in my school cafeteria asking for applicants. Somehow, the job title of Sandwich Artist appealed to my adolescent amateur vanity. The call came from Subway the day after I clicked Apply. The interview doubled as a tour. *This is where we keep the bread, this is where we keep the cheese.*

My Subway was on the corner of a strip mall, a small precipice of chipped cement steps hanging from the end of the sidewalk that dropped off beside its door. People frequently fell down the steps—opened the glass door; turned left biting into their foot-longs; and tumbled out of sight. It was an everyday scene from my position at the counter, where I performed my sandwich artistry. Countless complaints were made about the steps, but nothing was ever done. People fell down the steps and came back the next week for more. Once I looked up and witnessed a man trip gracefully, his meatball sub soaring from his fingers as he dove. He reached for it as he went down.

Every component of every sandwich was regulated. Cheese slices, pickles, ounces of meat, those sheaths of processed pink rounds clinging to paper. I'd fantasize about a job where I'd feed people, but here I merely stuffed them methodically. Many of the customers were regulars, many ate alone. I memorized their preferences but still asked every time, because it was policy. A Sandwich Artist always encouraged all options and add-ons. I learned to go through the motions, not expect anything. I rolled each sandwich neatly, identically.

My tag read SOMA—SANDWICH ARTIST. I wore it with soul-scalded shame. "What kind of name is *Soma*?" a surprising number of Subway customers asked me.

I stared blankly into the demanding eyes and closed mouths of the hungry.

Hunger filled the parking lot, stuffed the banana-yellow seats. Soccer teams, graduate students wiping mustard drips off textbook pages, silent broke couples. I was shocked by how many adults dated at Subway. Obvious internet encounters against the backdrop of Top 40 hits and the dark groans of the industrial dishwasher. Its door slid down, side handle pulled as if guiding the descent of a guillotine blade, the light on, signalling its work. Inferno noise. For the first few weeks I slammed the door and rapidly backed away. When the light changed, I released the door upward, the steam billowing and scalding water showering down. I avoided the edges of the door, gathering the scorched pans. A co-worker in her fifties who'd worked there for eight years muttered disdainfully at me, "Don't be so afraid—it's not *alive*." We never spoke. She knew I was just a kid, passing through. Years after I quit, I passed the window one night and saw her in there, wrapping a sandwich in the antiseptic light.

Subway closed at eleven. Around ten-forty, there was the final surge. Everybody who'd missed their dinner, who never ate dinner, who worked through dinner, who had nobody to eat dinner with. It was the sad, late-night adult version of a bagged lunch, but packed by a teenager in a tunic and name tag.

I had all the combinations memorized—my fingers knew the coordinates of the trays of jalapenos, shredded lettuce, wet pickles, brittle onion hoops. Mustard and mayonnaise in gooey cross-hatch. I composed each sandwich perfectly.

When I locked the door before cleanup there was always one last person, fifteen minutes or half an hour later, outside the glass, tapping hopefully. I held up my mop in apology, shook my head, and they slid back into the darkness.

My father and I are watching the History Channel when Josiah comes up the stairs. His curly hair tarred with sweat. I look over at my father, expecting knowing eye contact, at least a smile. Nothing. My father is the same with Josiah as he is with me: he never criticizes. Once when Josiah and I were entrenched in a fight, my father sent me an email comprised of a single sentence—*Just stop it because you will always have each other*—and never brought it up in person. My father doesn't give in; he gives up.

"Hi, Josiah!" he says, as if Josiah has just arrived from France. My father holds up a bag of no-name potato chips. "Soma's making chicken!"

"Thank you so much, Soma."

"You are welcome, Josiah."

When he'd called yesterday, my father had said, "Josiah's been up to less lately." I squeezed him with questions until he admitted that Josiah had stopped leaving the house. He had no idea why—well, there was that girl. What girl? The girl from the store. What store? Oh, you know, those stores

Josiah goes to for his games. What happened with the girl? Well, he didn't quite know about that but he thought I should come over.

Josiah gazes at the History Channel. Men in white leggings and boat-shaped hats. He fills his mouth with chips. Chews, holding an expression of disgust. Ruining his appetite for my dinner, I think angrily.

"Smells good," he says.

"Yeah."

"You do the thing with the lemon."

"Yeah."

"You make my potatoes."

"If you want."

He shrugs. He has my flatness when he's down and has taken a kick in the gut. His eyes on the screen, jaws and shoulders slackened.

I go into the kitchen and make Josiah's favourite potatoes. Fist-sized cool russets from the bottom of the cupboard. The peels spool onto the cutting board, smelling of turned dirt. I quarter them, parboil them, dry the chunks with a dishtowel so the oil will stick, peel and crush the garlic, roll the potatoes in the oil and garlic and rock salt and cracked black pepper. The oven pours its familiar baptismal heat at me, and I toss handfuls of the potatoes around the bird. Its skin a caramel glaze. I baste it, dripping fat on the potatoes. Hot fog of lemon and skin smoke. I tent the chicken with foil and lower the oven temperature to 350. Shut the oven. When I was a kid I loved this moment. Locking the flavours in with the heat, the beginning of alchemy.

Commercial break. My father mutes the TV and waits.

"Why do people feel entitled to rip each other's lives to

shreds with their bare fucking hands?" Josiah says to no one.

The chip bag crackles. Hands reach for salt, for deep-fry, for the next taste.

My father's slow sigh, sensible as wind: "They get upset."

Quietly, I descend the stairs.

Pass through the silent hall to Josiah's room, test the door. Enter.

The way I remember it. His bedroom since childhood, layered with selves. Posters from his gamer conventions, a miniature gumball machine, a poster of a character from a show I've never watched—a svelte woman in a tunic carrying a galactic Uzi, her soft-porn intergalactic thighs tensed, her secretive smile. I scan the desk and night table for a photo of the girl from the store who has banished my brother. He would never be so careless.

Josiah visited me at Subway all the time. My fellow Sandwich Artists got to know him, would shout out, "Your twin is here!" and laugh, because there was barely any sibling resemblance. His towering curls; my clipped-short cut. His long body stretched on the rack of adolescence; my compact build, shoulders like a boxer's without any effort. In the photographs, my mother looked most like Josiah, their mouths never quite closed, their matched chins with wishbone clefts.

"Hi," he'd say, as if we'd just met. He refused to learn to cook for himself. When I was working, he would either turn up at Subway or eat bowls of instant noodles.

At first he ordered sandwiches off the menu. Meatball subs and cold cuts. Most of the time I gave him his sandwiches for free. Everybody gave their friends free food. The longer I worked there, the more he customized his sandwiches.

"Your twin is here!" one of my fellow sandwich artists would yell. It was understood that I was the one who would always prepare his sandwich. He had a talent for coming during quiet times. Sometimes I wondered if he circled the block, watching.

"What kind of bread?"

"Cheese bread."

"Six-inch or foot-long?"

"Foot long."

I reached for the cold cuts. "What kind of sandwich?"

"I'll have three of the macadamia white-chocolate cookies."

"Sure. What kind of sandwich?"

"Could you put the cookies in the sandwich?"

The Subway was empty except for a guy in the corner who'd been drinking Pepsi refills for an hour. I nodded and lined up the cookies on the bread.

"And?"

"Honey mustard."

I painted over the cookies slowly. He frowned at me seriously.

"That it?"

"Could I get that broiled?"

Under the broiler the cookies melted with surprising rapidity, like a shape-shifting alien life form. The honey mustard sank into the molten dough and the bread crisped, then burned.

I dusted the thing with garlic salt, wrapped it in paper, and handed it to him.

I saw him take a bite as he crossed the parking lot. He turned and raised the sandwich above his head, and the three of us standing behind the counter raised our arms in answer, we laughed, we cheered.

I sort through the stack of computer language manuals on his desk. He did one year of community college, then dropped out. Fast to learn, fast to bore. He earned twenty grand last year from his games, he'd told me, proud. He never bought anything major. Once he told me he saved most of it, but never told me what for. I didn't ask. I hoped that one day he'd move out without any warning.

"What the fuck are you doing?"

When I turn to him, he looks resigned, as if I'm a character in one of his games, making a predictably futile move.

"Sorry."

"Dad tell you to do this."

"No."

"Find what you were looking for?"

His Levis spur-thin. His wrists angled gently outward. He could never throw a ball straight, came home from try-outs dry-gulping rejection. Lay down in the parking lot and refused to get into the car.

"Soma. What the hell are you doing, going through my stuff?"

"Dad told me. A girl?"

His laughter grills my cheeks.

"He said that?"

"Yeah. At the store?"

"The store."

"Yeah. The gamer store?"

"Oh god. You know he just makes stuff up, right, Soma?"

"Yeah, I know."

He crosses his arms.

"He's trying."

"I just can't do anything anymore," he says.

"What?"

"There's something wrong with me."

"No."

"I'm not like other people. Other people—they do things. They just do them. My friends, they move to other cities. Just go. Greg moved to Chicago. Lev moved to Edmonton. They don't even think. They just go. Like it's not even that big. Like just life. There's just something wrong with me. I can never be like people. Just thinking thinking thinking thinking *thinking*. You know. What the fuck is wrong with me? There's something wrong with us. We're not like other people. We're like her."

The things I should say: *You're my brother. You're the person I know best.*

But I was raised by Sally Jessy Raphael and Rosie O'Donnell with her Koosh balls firing soft meteors into my thirteen-year-old belly. By lists of ingredients, steps of preparation, recipes that guided me through.

So I say, "I think the chicken's ready."

He follows me upstairs.

My chicken is perfect, like always.

I run the knife through it silkily. Divide the wings and

drumsticks between us, spoon jus over the potatoes. Copper skin, twist of bone, shards of grease.

We eat. We never speak while we eat. Rituals so old we never learned them. Later, I'll put the bones in a plastic bag and leave them in the freezer for broth.

So when I speak, they look up at me like startled children.

"Dad," I say. "Josiah's going to come live with me. Until he feels better."

My father turns to me, then turns to Josiah. Josiah bites down on a drumstick. Cartilage breaks.

"Where'll he sleep? Your place is a cubbyhole." There's something I didn't expect in his face: the relief.

"It's just for a few months. Until he can find something else." *I can't fix you, but I can take you with me.*

"Well, then I guess that's that. Are there some more of these potatoes?" My father carries his plate to the stove and faces it for a long time. The scraping of the spoon in the pan, pushing around the caramelized spuds, the charred rosemary bundles and lemons swollen with juices.

I chew my feast, avoid my brother's eyes. Careful not to consume the bulk of his gratitude all at once. There are things that take years to eat. This is what we are. We can feed only on each other, salted and cured. It is hardest to be left behind.

Stargazer

AT NIGHT, YOUR STRAINED VOCAL CORDS FORM A glowing band around the moon. You do not know what you are asking for this time. Shapes assemble at the perimeter and call themselves fingertips, cheeks, inkblot torsos. They have been here before. People you love are recycling names the way the world recycles seasons. Bees with frequency, voices turn on spokes, slow in the days, adrenal dive through the green substrata, decade roulette, but what is the true indicator of new life? The future sits across from you in the greasy spoon, saws into pancakes with ketchup on top, wields a steak knife, lectures you about making better choices, the long hall of unintended consequences. And if you can. If you looked harder, it would come to you, if you could just focus for once, this wouldn't be so hard, clavicle and tracery of eyes would make themselves present, no diagnostic mist this time. Shutters tumble around your fingers, rising in the darkness. You understand something about tone, about how to lie down in a throat and fall asleep like you own the place. You have always excelled at Rorschach tests, can read suggestion in the shift of shoulders, some air seeping from a mouth at a specific tilt, a thread you can grab and twist. You learned this

73

from growing up in a city that floats in a cloud chamber. A mimic fish spreading over eyes, cheeks, collarbones. Every face, a display plate on a simple white stand. Stargazer. When you were small, a big kid taught you how to cut a slit down the belly of a green blade of grass, break open with your breath, and make music, and it was the first weapon you ever made. You aimed it at the sky, blasted an escape hatch. But now there is a shift, a settling. It's dark. Portrait game. Voices turn on spokes, more slowly now. The faces carousel around the small warm pyramid created by your hands. Milky light seeps through the seams in commuter traffic. When you narrow your eyes, your fatigue blurs into the tactile future. Halos, overexposures cast into the deep pools of other minds. Butterflies pressed behind eyelids. Drape all the mirrors. Learn how to pray.

Who You Start With Is Who You Finish With

CHARNA

If you asked me where we are from, I would tell you it doesn't matter. It only matters where you are going. Where are you going? Wherever you can, and sometimes you have no choice in the matter. That ship everyone's talking about at shul after services, all those poor people crowded at the edges, looking out at the water, hopeful fools, turned away everywhere, and they keep going looking for a place that will take them in. Not here—that much is obvious now. Sorry. You have to go. The Prime Minister William Lyon Mackenzie King is a Jew-hater, my father, my *tateleh*, says. What a monster. I wish I could burn his house down. Starting with his fake smile. You learn how to read a smile. There's all the stuff that's happening on the outside of people and then everything that's happening inside. Those are completely different things. It's important not to get them confused. They can have nothing to do with each other, the outside and the inside. You just never know about people. I bet those people on the ship know that. I hope they do. Where will they go now? The Arctic Circle? How many Jews are up there? We're all hiding from something.

No, that's not true. Some aren't hiding at all. Some people just sit there, watching others suffer. You can call me bitter, but I know a thing or two about people. My sister said to me: Charna, you're only twenty-four, too young to be so bitter! Bitter, me? *Nu*? You don't need to be bitter, you just need to listen to the stories of what's happening now. You just need to think about that ship with its dining rooms and blankets on beds and children, stuck up on an iceberg like an ornament on a cake with buttercream frosting. You know they're sending that ship back to Germany and those people will probably die, and don't call me bitter, instead look at their faces, look at the faces of the people who know. Those who are already on their way.

This writer, Isaac Bashevis Singer—he really knows how to tell a story. People are people are people. The way he writes, as if he carries a pad and pencil around with him every day of his life. He writes Yiddish just the way my father, Tateleh, and his friends talk. Tateleh is always having people over. Their Yiddish, guttural and rapid, so different than their English, a stiff plod. They drink the brightest amber tea from the samovar, small glasses set out on the table like stars hanging in the room at the level of their hands while they tell each other the news, direct the constellations of facts. Singer writes about pogroms but, oh, if I asked Tateleh about all that, the look I would get. "Where are you from, Tateleh?" is a question I will never ask. From a place to leave and never go back, even for a visit. I drift in and out of the room, stand at the door, and listen in for whatever scraps I can get. I watch my cousin Mordecai standing by another door, also listening. Zev Guttman's sister's family is on that ship and we are hoping the circle of men will say something about it. Mordecai stares across the room at me. Half in shade. Sickle of cheekbone. Perfect Mordecai, who does not drive on Saturdays, who smiles at me because he knows my secret, that I am dating a *goy*, a man who has the nerve not to be a Jew. Mordecai isn't a blood cousin, we have none here; he's the son of one of the men in Tateleh's tea circle.

One of the older men says, "What could we do, swim out to the ship and throw bread up its sides?" Many people from shul have sent letters about their families trapped over there. It's been getting harder and harder for a few years for families to come here to Winnipeg. The old man mutters a prayer and everybody repeats. My lips and tongue moving through the Hebrew too, before I even notice.

Someone answers, "The bread would only fall back down and get ruined in the ocean."

Another man says, "I would catch it in my mouth!"

My father mimes swimming to shore, teeth gripping invisible bread, frantic dog-paddling.

Laughter dips and fades like a fire dying out.

The Singer stories came from a friend of Tateleh's who often goes back and forth across the border to the States. My father and mother first came to the States when they left their shtetl, their village, in eastern Ukraine, then moved up here. I don't know why—what makes Canada any better? I read the Singer stories all in one burst. Tateleh read the stories quickly, and then left them under a stack of newspapers. The stories are set in the 1600s. There are very few Jews left in the shtetl, because of very awful pogroms.

There is a messiah who is probably not a messiah, and a girl who is possessed by a dybbuk, a demon. Once a dark spirit is in you, it takes a very long time for it to get out, and you're probably a *bissl* crazy forever. All very dramatic. Tateleh buys newspapers in both Yiddish and English. I had to explain to Louis, the boy I'm seeing, mild Louis tall as a lamppost, that the Yiddish is not Hebrew. He laughed. "It all looks the same!" I tried to explain to him that Yiddish is the language people speak, not the language we use to pray. Louis and his family just talk English. His mother knows about us and she is unhappy he's dating a Yid, of course, but did not tell him to stop. He is so persistent. She must know that about her only son. Louis asks me to say words in Yiddish—door, house, father—and I do: *tir, hoyz, tateh*. He asks me to say words in Hebrew, insists playfully, pressing me to the edges of my temper that he is beginning to know well, like feeling for the walls of a dark room. "Teach me how, Charna," he teases me. Louis promises several times a week that his mother will meet me soon. Tateleh does not know about Louis, of course. He has warned me: do not be surprised that anybody hates you for being a Jew. But he has also said, nothing can change where you come from. We are from shtetls, the Jewish villages, where most people we know are from. I was born soon after they arrived here, but I often feel as if I'm from elsewhere. After all, who can remember their own birth?

In shul there are many stories about what's happening over there. Before prayers there is the real story: the gossip. Zev Guttman's skin is fragile as the cloth of his old tallit he brought with him from Berlin, and I know there is no good news about the ship. There have been more pogroms. In cities where they're supposed to be civilized. "It's 1939! What is this? This meshuga garbage," Tateleh spits. I take comfort in his disbelief until a friend of his says, "Why should we be surprised by anything? Isn't that is why we are here and not there?" In shul Tateleh is far from me, in the men's section, and I watch him out of the corner of my eye during the Amidah. As he prays, his bulk sways freely forward and back, a black bear suspended on wires. I have never wondered what he prays for, until today. He is massive, my father, never cuts his beard, rough yarn that spools from his chin. My sister says he's depressing to be around, that I should ask for help finding a husband and move out of the apartment. "Charna, it's time to go," she tells me. Silent prayer is the part of service I love most. When a building full of people think the same words at the same time, the air shimmers with the vowels trapped in their lungs. Invisible people wander among us, blow in our mouths and ears. Zev Guttman looks like he's holding his breath, like he might faint at any moment, and I close my eyes, let the words float me along.

SOMA

A few days before my grandmother Charna's fifth yahrzeit —the fifth anniversary of her death in the Hebrew calendar—I go away with my partner, Melanie, to an island up the coast. The ferry cuts through the hard black wax of the Pacific and my body moves toward a nameless heaviness it always does at this time of year, end of summer, when Grandma Charna died, the pale heat edging toward a finish.

We booked the trip months ago and, when I realized that it overlapped with her yahrzeit, I hesitated, then left the dates alone. A change is better than a rest, is something she said. We all have our meshugas, is another thing she said. We all have our craziness, crazies, we are all the craziness, sometimes. Nobody more or less, just taking turns. I have the Kaddish downloaded on my iPhone. I meant to print it out at the office but forgot, so my iPhone prayer will have to do the job. Moments like this make me feel like a pretend-Jew or, what I actually am, a half-Jew. The joke I tell people when they ask if it's my father or mother: it's the left side. I've been listening to the prayer on my earbuds during my hour-long work commute for weeks. The riddled lilt of the mourner's prayer. This year, I decided to memorize it for Grandma Charna, not read it as I've done the previous four years. Memorizing it has been harder than I predicted, the sequences too complex. I thought it was Hebrew until I googled and found out it's actually Aramaic. A language even more distant from me than Yiddish, my grandma Charna's birth tongue, a language she rarely spoke in front of me, tried not to pass on to her children, save them from that clipped, giveaway accent in the years after the Holocaust. A shifting blend of German, Hebrew, Polish, Ukrainian—the mishmash everyone spoke before everything changed.

Mameh loshen, mother tongue.

Inside the ferry, we get hot chocolates, watch the Pacific, its ambling slurry. The island is three ferries away from Vancouver, each ferry crossing a deeper relief. Carrying us away from the daily drain of our jobs. How can this coast be simultaneously so beautiful and so polluted? If its insides were shown, its heavy-metal count and creatures strangled by chemicals, it would be hideous. This is the kind of thing I say that makes Melanie grimace and say, "Why do you have to be so negative about *everything*?" "It's not negative if it's true," I argued once, and she said, "Oh my god, you *have* to write that down." I drink my shitty salty hot chocolate while Melanie dozes against the window. I inspect the surface of the brown liquid. There are black shimmering patches like gasoline. What do they put in this stuff? I fish a *Globe and Mail* from between the seats. The cover story is about a town in Wisconsin where a neo-Nazi group is organizing a march. Photos of Jewish adults and children have been taped on telephone poles throughout the town. Similar groups are popping up across the States, the article goes on to say. The mayor has voiced his criticism of the group and assured the town that every effort is being made to contain the planned rally. Contain? I feel derision sparkle in my fingertips. I hear Grandma Charna: What do you think they're doing, *planning a birthday party for a child*? Her laugh an unstable creature. They think they can stop this? With a declaration of disapproval? People like this, they never go away. They won't stop at anything. Nothing they won't do. They won't stop at anything. I'm glad she isn't alive to see this—the photos of spray-painted gravestones in Ottawa and Winnipeg and Toronto, the Rabbis receiving anonymous phone threats, the chanting crowds of furious young white men. This surreal resurgence. I examine the men's faces in the black-and-white newspaper images. I set my index finger over their mouths, gingerly, testing for heat. Who are you and what do you want? Purity. We want purity. The ocean moves outside, a dark brain, deep folds of shadow and light. Melanie doesn't understand about Grandma Charna. Her family gets along in a way that confounds me. At first I thought they were pretending to be that normal. During the first few months we knew each other, I waited for the big reveal of dysfunction. Spoiler: there was none. You would never guess, meeting Melanie, that she did half of medical school, dropped out to become a vet when she became obsessed with a rescue dog. When I tried to explain to her a little about Charna, Melanie said, slowly, careful not to offend: "Sounds like she had a lot of baggage." I laughed. Baggage. Understatement of the century. Melanie's family is a mix of Swedish and Scottish.

She's asked me a few times, "Where's your family from again?"

"Ukraine," I said. "Near the Black Sea." I repeated what Grandma Charna said to me: "I don't know a lot about it."

Early on, Melanie was surprised. "But how can you just not *know*? This is the twenty-first century, aren't there records?" It's hard to explain, the Holocaust and pogroms and back and back and back.

"Too much to get into."

I told her once that the government didn't even release any records until the nineties, and she dropped the subject. They never met. Grandma Charna would either have loved her or torn her to shreds. Probably both. Melanie awakens, shifts, leans against me. She takes the *Globe and Mail* out of my hands.

"Stop reading that stuff," she says.

I wrap my arms around her. "Why? It's what's happening."

Her yawn slurs her words. "Too much. It's too much. We're almost at the island. Can't you take a break?" I curl my fingers through her hair. I love the texture of her hair, the dense coils. When wet, heavy as metal springs.

"It's just a newspaper article," I murmur softly, trying to cover my defensiveness with sleepiness. I slide my hand down her neck, to her bra strap. "Don't," she says, leans forward and takes the *Globe* with her, pushes it onto the ground. "We should never have gone away during this yardzite thing," she says.

"Yahrzeit," I correct automatically.

"I know, yahrzeit." She rolls back and forth in her seat, slurs like a pirate: "Yahhrrrrrrrrrrrrrr-zite. Yahrrrrrrrr matey zite."

Here she is, again, in my arms, intolerable, refusing-to-get-it, consoling. "How much do you love me?" she asks, falling asleep again, and I tell her.

When the ferry docks on the tiny island, there are sounds like fire smacking ice, the hissing and popping of a rough entry. We unpack our stack of cut-offs and T-shirts. Her warm hand on my bare shoulder. "You're going to be moody this whole trip, aren't you?" she asks, and I turn and kiss her. She knows about the yahrzeit but not about the Kaddish in Aramaic on my phone, a glaring exception in an endless loop of R 'n' B and acoustic covers. She would recede into disapproving silence if I told her I'd listened to the prayer on repeat over these past few weeks, mouthing along to the ancient words, the pulse of vowels in a minor key. Words that I recite cautiously, laboriously, like reciting a character's words in a foreign play. I am that crazy lady on the bus, meshuga, rehearsing death, hunched in a plastic seat, the competing voice intoning from the speaker system, *This*

train is bound for Waterfront Station. I have not told her why
I am so upset about this yahrzeit, can feel my body stiffen-
ing in anticipation before a fall or jump—I am now the age
my grandma Charna was the year the Holocaust ended and
there was, officially, nowhere to return to. But what could
they even have known, then? Grandma Charna withheld so
much, it's easy to feel, sometimes, like I'm making it all up.

The ocean is at the foot of the cliff behind our cabin, with
a trail straight down to Pacific black.

CHARNA

At the kiddush lunch at shul, there are many stories about
everyone's families trapped in Europe. I get up and wander into the corner alone. A pile of old prayer books rests
on a table. I should take one of those siddurs back home,
begin a daily routine. My sister Hannah dragged me to her
prayer circle six months ago, and the woman who leads
her group spoke passionately about her siddur as her best
friend, always giving the *best* advice. This is the kind of
thing that summons my snark from the lizard seed of my
brain. My sister had looked at me hard, stunned, when I
told her about the seriousness of my feelings for Louis after the group, and then she said, very slowly, "What is your
long-term plan?" When I glared, she said, "No, it's not that,
I just don't want you to go through pain. Eventually, you
will have to make a choice." Nobody in our shul marries
non-Jews. Why would anyone marry a goy. *Just look at what
they've done to us.* Now, I'm standing holding the siddur,

and Hannah comes up. Successfully married to bland Joshua, and excruciatingly pregnant. She puts all ten of her fat hard fingers in my hair and whispers very close to my face, "What are you thinking about, scowling here in the corner holding a prayer book like a meshuga lady, the end of the world? Come and talk." She wants to know how Tateleh is doing and I tell her about his friends and the joke about the dog swimming. I think about that dog, tired in the middle of the Atlantic. I expect her to sigh and shake her head—*like a bunch of old ladies, sitting around gossiping*—but instead she puts a hand on her explosive belly, and says, "Yes we must all be careful these days. It's different for you, Charna, you were born after they came here, but I remember." She was five when they came and has told me scraps over the years—the boat full of sickness, the vague shapes of the many faces from before, Tateleh's mother and sisters.

Then: "You spend too much time with old men. Old people, and that goy Louis. I'm going to hunt him down and attack him from behind." She screeches and grabs at the soft folds of my stomach, chases me away with a pelvic thrust.

Hannah's prayer group meets in a different home every week. Her best friend since Hebrew school, Basha, is the host this week. From the way Basha looks at me slyly, I know she knows about my relationship with Louis. A person like her will take a story and run with it to see how far it can get her. I fear her judgment and her love of advertising in equal amounts. The other women rub Hannah's stomach like a charmed stone.

"What have you been up to, Charna?" one of them asks me, and I answer that last night I enjoyed spending the evening working on the *parashah* for tonight's group. She looks confused and glances at Hannah.

"Didn't Hannah tell you what this group is for now?"

I shake my head.

"We write letters." Basha takes out a book of addresses of members of parliament, and mayors of cities from where we are in Manitoba all the way east. They've been gathering and writing these letters for weeks now.

Dear Sir: As members of the Jewish community and as Canadian citizens, we are writing to express our deep concern regarding the situations of our community's families currently residing in areas of Europe...

We ask for your kind consideration of the extremity of circumstances...

As taxpaying citizens...

While we write and fold, Hannah begins to sing a wordless melody. Spirals, widens, never resolves. The prayer continues for a long time until we fall into silence, like a woman dropping the end of a rope to the floor. I see that Basha, normally coy and mercurial, is crying. I wonder where her family's relatives are. Germany, I think. Things are getting worse quickly. Hannah's hand moving mechanically back and forth across where she is full of her child, Tateleh's first grandchild. He shouted when he found out, a ripcord pulled at the root of his throat. The baby will be named according to our Ashkenazi tradition, with the initials of the names taken from family who have passed away. I asked him, will the initials be your parents' initials?

We have been trained to never talk about the past, but sometimes it's just the natural thing to say—what were his parents' names? A door is closed between before and now. There and here. The door cannot be opened. A few things have drifted through, a melody and the scent of loss. Yiddish. My sister's pen moving across the page, occasionally slipping back to cup the heartbeat of her child.

The ship never arrived. Changed its course out there. They would not even allow it to dock its thoughts here. So we hear. For a long time it has been very difficult, but now there will be no more families coming. I have a strange thought: now, it is only us.

I have never even seen the ocean.

There is much more in the Yiddish newspaper than the English newspaper about the new laws, the roundups, the bureaucratic delays that have lockjawed into refusal. Canada is not letting Jews in. Europe is not letting Jews out. There is a space in between, a space between us, so deep, and I heard some of the old women at shul talking about it, one started weeping, "It's the same as before, the same as before, but now worse," and a friend of Tateleh's pulled me toward the table laden with dishes of potatoes and fish so I wouldn't hear any more. I say to Hannah, "What can I do?" Hannah answers, "There's nothing we can do but be glad we are not there." Our mother died of influenza when I was four, her body not equipped against the illnesses on this new continent, and we never speak of this either. In my childhood, when Hannah and I went to the deli to scoop herring from the barrels that smelled like an open sewer, the women stared at us. They judged Tateleh for never re-marrying. A man with two daughters could not be without a wife. But he avoided, first by hiding with us all under a prayer shawl woven from his grief, then by spending all of his time working. Many people from shul had told me, sug-gestively, your tateleh works too hard. What does he do with his time? They suspected he was seeing a secret lover, or a goy, but no. I listened to his nighttime prayers. Moth-erless, I was sad, but also freer than other girls. He never forced me to do anything. These days, his friends come and gather often in our apartment. The samovar is cut with dark ghosts of trees. The amber tea. I sit in my room and try to read the siddur I took from shul. I whisper the bless-ing for sleep. How is it that when I say these words, they are supposed to make something happen? I must remember to tell Tateleh that it doesn't matter if he doesn't know the names of his parents; we can name Hannah's baby for our mother. But this is useless to say. He knows the names of his parents and cannot bear to say them aloud, to repeat what he was forced to leave behind. He reads the newspa-per, fingers burrowed in his hair, shoulders hunched, brows carved. I let him be.

SOMA

Grandma Charna predicted her own death. She said, "This is my last year. I've decided." She chuckled. She nev-er laughed at jokes, only at truths. She was often saying things like that—things that, at the time, felt out of left field, uncalled for, too dark, but looking back were big and true and right. After I graduated from university, the big recession hit the States, then swept across the border to Canada, and she said to me, "Be careful, the Great Depression created the Holocaust." I did what I always did: nodded and fell silent and wondered at her worries, the giant quiet wellspring, always blooming, always replenishing, under everything. It's hard to say if that is what made her feel unknowable, or if it was her intelligence, her penetrating read of people. Probably a bit of both. When she disagreed with you, she would look deep in your eyes, as if waiting for the next thought to reveal itself; I used to shut my eyes and whine, "Stop it!" When I was little, she told me often that people are limited, so it's best to expect as little as you wish to be disappointed, and I believed her. I believed everything she said.

I listen to Melanie get the coffee going and open all the doors wide downstairs and I lie in bed googling "alt right" and "fascism" and "canada" on my phone. I need to know the details. A rabbi in Surrey, a half-hour drive from our apartment, has awakened to find her door anointed with red swastikas. I hear Grandma Charna's voice, whispering in my ear, "Maybe they'll poison her little dog too." I never argued with her pessimism. It would have felt like theft. She had full claim to the past; I was history's blind passenger, ferried along in her blood vessels. An editorial on the CBC website laments that we are in a new age of fascism, this year in the twenty-first century, to be remembered as the starting point of a dark spiral. A few of my friends have reposted an article comparing the restrictions against Syrian refugees to Canada's refusal to admit Jews before the Holocaust. When do people know that something is beginning? How do people know when to leave? Where is the moment, the sign? A symbol or a door? A scream in the street? No one in our family has ever been back to eastern Ukraine. If I were to go, I would be the first to go back since everyone was run out or killed. Grandma Charna taught her children: there is nothing to go back for. We are not really from there—what we came from is gone. So, are we from nowhere? She read the newspaper every morning; I got my obsession with news from her. The same photo of the swastika on the rabbi's door floods my Facebook newsfeed, a column of bent spiders, a chain, interlocked feet and teeth, unbreakable. Melanie calls me from downstairs. I met her a year after Grandma Charna's death, just after the first yahrzeit. Grief had split me. There's a string of neo-Nazi protests planned for cities across Canada next week. I put the phone away.

Melanie is frying up a pound of bacon when I come down the stairs. She piles it with avocado slices. There are buns and grapefruit, halved, with brown sugar in wet mounds. We drive around the island, stopping at the food co-op, beaches, the two harbours, the store that sells knee-high boots and cans of gas to fishermen. She knows how to distract me, stares sharply at me sideways while driving, and says, "What are you brooding about?" She regrets going on this trip during the yahrzeit. I can tell. My memories of doing things with Grandma Charna are so few; I only remember our conversations. She didn't like the things other people liked—going to movies, going for walks, visiting the ocean. She liked to sit in their tiny apartment and gossip, argue. Grandpa Louis reading his newspaper in the background. She didn't like to talk about being Jewish. When I was around twelve or thirteen, she sat me down and told me the tradition for naming babies, the tradition she had used to name my father and his sisters—take the first letters of names from previous generations who had passed on. So her children didn't have the Yiddish or Hebrew names she and her sister had, but they kept the letters. The names of her mother's and father's murdered families were woven in there, like a secret code. When she told me this, my brain recorded it like a tape, but I stared at her, silent. She probably wondered if she had a mute for a granddaughter. A spy or a sponge. She kept a Talmud in the guest room, but in all the years I visited, I never saw it move. The overlap in the Venn diagram of our lives. I remember her voice, cracking slightly, saying, so formally and strangely, to me, "In my culture, *which is Jewish*, this is how we name the children." Which is Jewish. As if she had to defend, explain, or qualify herself. It took me until my late teens to put the pieces together, go looking on my own. After drifting through religious studies courses in undergrad, where I listened to students argue about how many men wrote the Bible, I took a Holocaust class, and when we learned about the online Holocaust registry, I logged on and typed in Grandma Charna's family's last name and the city on the Black Sea close to our shtetl. She would never say the name of the shtetl. An endless list of people appeared on the screen, with photos and dates. Every shtetl in the region had been raided, the inhabitants massacred or marched to camps, I read. I scrolled down and down and down, my mind loosening, swarming, darkening. During my next visit, I told her about the Holocaust class, and she tapped my middle knuckle with her index finger. "What's the use of something like that? It will make you sick!" Things she left me: the tendency to keep secrets; a mood surfacing like a hundred-year-old whale from the ocean; a very old copy of Isaac Bashevis Singer stories, margins webbed with her notes, her name in Yiddish script on the inside cover. Yiddish script is read backwards, resembles the footprints of spiders, if spiders had footprints. Isaac Bashevis Singer, her favourite writer. I tried to read the stories. They're full of Jewish clichés, like something out of *Fiddler on the Roof*—wanderers uttering platitudes, rabbis peddling lost worlds, the oppression by the Russians. And the women—always really sad or crazy. She said, "What's the use of talking about the past? What's done is done." Melanie and I eat fish and chips on a restaurant's falling-apart plywood balcony, tear off the golden skins, drip grease on our shirts, wander around at low tide ruining our sneakers with black sand reeking of fish eggs, and she buys me an ugly hand-shaped mug from a woman living in a tent behind the grocery co-op.

Melanie wraps her arms around my waist, says, "I'm so glad we're here."

"Here we are," I answer.

"Try not to think too much," she says.

Melanie is a deep sleeper. I slip out of bed, down the stairs, and out of the cabin. I go down to the water. I need to practice.

Tomorrow will be Grandma Charna's yahrzeit. The churning of the water among loose stones, the continuous replacement of the shore, a moving finish line. I used to think that people in our family were dark people, brooding people. Damaged goods. It took me such a long time to realize that it was something that happened to us, something from the outside that should never have happened at all. Who can say: where we come from, everyone was killed, massacred in their villages that no longer exist? Piled in trenches dug by their neighbours, doused with gasoline. And in winter, the ground too frozen to penetrate, the people herded into barns and the barns set on fire. The report released in the nineties says that the people were seen waving from their windows, flames made of Jews. What the hell am I supposed to do with that? Maybe it's better not to know. Better not to talk about it. Better not to dig things up. That's what they thought, pretenders at being from nowhere. I can go on and on about this stuff, need to remind myself to rein it in. Something I can say, though, is that I'm not as bitter as Charna. I'm different. Don't be bitter—it will make you hard. You'll push people away. She told me, before I could understand, that *those people* were murderers. Before I knew anything else about her, I knew there was something I could never repair. The wind blows frozen off the ocean, though it's late summer. Night makes the water unforgiving, impenetrable. I take my iPhone out of my pocket and scan the Kaddish again. Too cold to practise. If Melanie wakes up, she'll panic that I'm gone. My thumb coaxes the text downward.

A loose stone under my foot and my hand flails and springs open. The screen a white apparition under the sheen of water. I'm on my knees, scrambling in the water. The screen goes dead. I smash the glass against a stone and stomp, shivering and shaking, to the cabin. Even my stupid smartphone prayer, I've failed at.

I cannot sleep and then, when I do, I dream about a woman who is not my grandmother, in a room with cement walls, a lightless room, maybe a bunker, talking on an old-fashioned phone with a spiral cord connected directly to the wall, pleading with the person on the other end of the line. I am standing in the corner of the room, unable to intervene, powerless. I do not recognize this woman but then I do: it's Charna, but much, much younger, around the same age I am now, disguised by decades. Her fear balloons hot and fills the room. She is pleading into the phone: "She needs to know her great-grandmother's Hebrew name." She is talking about me. I wake up, fighting with the sheets that lasso my body, and stumble down the stairs from the sleeping loft. My back and my legs ache. At the bottom of the stairs, I pitch forward into a pool, elbows knocking, forehead slamming into the floor. My right leg is a river of electric pain. I curl up on the floor, and Melanie comes running down the stairs. I see her plaid pyjamas and planetary blue eyes. She rolls me onto my side, extends my arm under the side of my head, repeats, "Breathe." Her voice, distant, screams my name. I feel her veterinarian fingers do all the right things—check my throat, dig into my pulse. "We need to go to the hospital," she's saying. I laugh. "There's no hospital on this island." My laughter is incoherent and balms my pulsating muscles. There is a rip in my spine and heat comes rushing through. I wait until the pain settles, and Melanie helps me reluctantly to the couch after I pull myself up onto my feet on my own, stagger forward. "I'm fine, I'm fine." She wants to me stay there, on the floor, until we can know I'm not injured, wants to lie against my back, cradles me gingerly.

My whole life, people have told me I have an old soul. What will I be like when I am old?

CHARNA

For a time, when I was a small child, I hardly went to school at all. I hated the orderliness, the English, the rude shout of the bell, the way the English teacher drew out my name: *Cha-ahr-na*. I preferred the Yiddish of our home. So when I wanted some time to myself, I left our apartment in the morning and went to sit on the synagogue steps. If someone passed and asked me what I was doing there, I would report confidently, "My tateleh is inside saying Kaddish for my dead mother," and the person would nod and continue walking. Nobody wants to interfere in a family's mourning. Stick fingers into the grease trap of private ritual. *Mishpocheh* is strange, but untouchable. Family. My strategy worked for quite a while. A number of times, my father's friends from shul passed and raised their eyebrows at my response, knowing I was lying. But they did not question me. My small body perched on the stone steps of our shul. "My tateleh is inside reciting Kaddish for my mother, who has died," was my refrain. Of course I knew the words to the Kaddish, heard it every week at shul. We are so used to death that everyone knows the mourner's prayer. Or we are so in awe of death that we mark its passing as often as we can, while we meet on this side of life. One day I was sitting on the steps while my classmates were taking a geography test about the prairies when I saw my tateleh's brimmed black hat at the end of the street. Here it comes—his hat like a solar eclipse. He never walked this direction during the day. He stopped at the foot of the steps, looked up at me, bowed, and recited, *Yitgadal v'yitkadash sh'mei raba b'alma di-v'ra,* and continued until I joined in. I yelled the *ameins.* My small high voice rebounded from the stone. I shook and I shook and I shook. My father carried me back to our apartment on his back.

Hannah hosts the next meeting of her group at Tateleh's. The apartment she has with her husband, Joshua, is tiny and prepared for the baby, a cradle beside their bed with a blessing nailed above it. Tateleh locks himself in his room with a peace offering of cake and applesauce and tea. Hannah rushes around and opens all the windows. "You two live like a couple of old spinsters," she hisses at me. "I don't know how you'll ever raise a family of your own." I fill in the next words myself: *with that man.* Marrying a non-Jewish man is an act of leaving—my marriage would not even be recorded at shul. I will be an invisible Jew if I let Louis have his way. And I want him to. Sometimes when Louis holds me, I am full of dread, and then flooded by an unbearable joy. Basha's women arrive shouting news. The paper and envelopes and book of addresses are set out on the table. The work begins. Basha speaks loudly about her sister, who is getting married soon. There is also news that Cousin Mordecai will be married next year. At some point, my father comes into the kitchen for more tea. I watch his hazel eyes scan the growing stacks of letters. He takes too long to find the tea leaves, pack them with his thumb into the tin ball, and drop it into the cup and watch it sink into the water like a fishing lure. I pray for Basha, that *yente* cow, to stop talking when she says to Tateleh, "Yezekhiel, we are so pleased to hear the men's study group is helping with the fundraiser next month." The group is led by Zev Guttman, who comes every time to Tateleh's tea circle.

My father turns slowly. "*Nu?*"

Basha explains eagerly. "Raising funds for the Jewish Congress to bring people over. The conditions are getting worse—more violence, nobody can get out now." She goes on and on. I concentrate on writing to avoid his glance. I pray for Basha to stop talking.

I hear his sigh like a rotted-out step giving way.

"Are you going to contribute?" Basha asks.

Silence. My father says, "No." He drags the tea ball around the cup.

Hannah shakes her head at Basha but Basha does not know when to stop. "Why not? It would be lovely to see you there."

My father says, lifting his cup: "And what are you hoping to accomplish?" Basha says: "To bring people to safety."

Tateleh: "What you are doing is not that."

Basha: "What?"

I look at my hands.

Tateleh: "You do not know."

Basha: "Pardon me?"

Tateleh: "You are not going to help anyone. You are only making things worse for all of us, rocking the boat, drawing attention to us. Why risk making things worse? The same could happen here...very easily, the same could happen here. *Tsuris.*" Troubles.

When I look up at Basha, she is white and the women are silent, staring at Tateleh.

Tateleh: "What happens happens. We take care of our families."

Basha: "But that is *meshugeh*—"

Hannah says, "Tateleh, we are only trying. If no good comes of it, then—" She raises her hands.

Basha: "What are we supposed to do, pray?"

Tateleh, walking out of the room, voice staying in the room longer than the body: "You have never seen what they do to Jews."

SOMA

She would have liked this. Because she liked to do things on her own, and only in her own way.

I go down to the ocean.

I say Kaddish for her in that light generated by the ocean at dawn, even though nobody is supposed to say this prayer alone. The stones at the shore shake with quiet.

I'm worried I won't be able to do this without my phone, but I know the words by heart, the words I have prepared, practised. When I try to remember the beginning, the rest are there. The prayer unspools from my tongue. Only life upon all of us. Mighty be the name. The ocean marks time in the background.

This is what I want, and I take it. This is mine. I learned this from her: to be unapologetic. To take what I want. To not wait for what is already mine.

I thought I would feel her now, but I don't feel her at all. She is missing from the spaces between the ancient vowels that crowd the edge. I listen for her there. The sky hangs, a scrubbed shell.

I send the words to her.

Nothing comes back.

CHARNA

Every night before I sleep, I think about that ship on its way back to Europe. In my mind, it moves swiftly, soundlessly, barely brushing the waves. Godforsaken people. No news of arrival, no place of leaving. The news is so bad and then there is only a stomach-sick quiet that drags on. No going back. *Gornisht helfn.* Beyond help. There is a revolving door inside my tateleh that never stops moving. How long does it take to cross the ocean? Forever and no time at all.

SOMA

Melanie keeps asking me if I want to go home early, see a doctor on the mainland about my leg. No, I insist, I'm fine. She inspects my knee and ankle, mutters, "But you were in so much pain, it doesn't make *sense*." Nerve pain, she tells me. Early indications of sciatica? I don't tell her about the dream about Grandma Charna. I don't want to freak her out. When I tell her I tripped on a log and dropped my iPhone on the beach, she says, surprising me, "Good, maybe now you'll stop googling all that crazy shit about Nazi psychos in Surrey," and slides pancakes onto my plate, and I realize she's been checking my browser history or watching me while I scroll obsessively after dinner. "Can I use your phone?" I ask, and she doesn't answer, passes me the maple syrup. While I eat, the dream replays on endless loop in my mind. Why does Grandma Charna want me to know her mother's Hebrew name? I know little about her parents. They fled the anti-Jewish raids near the Black Sea. Left their families behind. That's just what people did, thinking their families would follow or they could return for them later. Nobody could have known what was coming—the borders closing, all the Jews registered, the liquidation. Thousands marched in circles around icy fields for weeks, to reduce the numbers. The Atlantic, the new wall between life and death. Don't bother waiting for the sea to part; get a fake visa instead. I know that her mother died young and that her father lived on for a long time, died from a heart attack in synagogue, was a very religious man. "He died while reciting the Kaddish, of course," Grandma Charna told me, and chuckled. It was often impossible to tell if she was joking. I don't even know his first name. They all made up fake English names when they arrived anyway. Her sister Hannah was also devout, became more religious in her later years, and lived between Jerusalem and Winnipeg. Grandma Charna was the black sheep. She never talked about the controversy created by her marriage to Grandpa Louis. In those days, it was unheard of, to marry outside. People fled and kept to themselves, especially after the Holocaust. Grandma Charna had her five babies. Born during and after the Holocaust—her second baby, my father, in 1945. "Your father's birth ended the Holocaust," she told me when I was six or seven, and chuckled. Humour, how we give and keep at the same time. How we make each other remember. Melanie loves to drive down every side road when we travel. Our little hatchback jounces over stones and potholes, and my leg aches gently. I shift in my seat, away from the ache. Melanie points out a minor waterfall, a field of alpacas bred for sweaters for trust-fund nomads.

"I love it that people just sort of move to these islands to check out and make stuff," she says. "Don't you think we'd be happier if we lived here and not in the city? They must be desperate for vets who would move here. Do you want to go for a walk?" She points to a sign. "It's to the beach that's supposed to have the best view of the channel."

I smile at her. "Are you trying to refocus my attention onto something constructive outside of myself?" I tease.

"Yes." She hesitates. "Is your leg going to be okay?"

"I'll be fine."

We start off down the path toward the ocean.

CHARNA

Hannah's baby comes fast. The midwife unravels the umbilical cord deftly from her neck, slaps her back, declares her here. I crawl into bed with my sister, her body an empty glove. Tateleh, when he runs into the room, is like I've never seen him before. "*Baruch hashem,*" Tateleh says. "*Baruch hashem,*" Hannah's Joshua echoes. Their voices full of awe, their eyes underwater caves flooded with wonder. "*Baruch hashem,*" I repeat obediently. I eye the tiny scarlet face. Blank eyes. No one in our family can come here anymore, but here you are. A magic trick. A human from nothing. Did you fly through a tunnel under the ocean, above the stars? Did you travel with a visa issued by G-d? Who did you meet at the right cocktail party, who you could slip a stack of bills for a safe passage? Did you say at the border between life and death that you are not a Jew? Did an angel change your name in a registration book while the man with the pen had his back turned? Did you fly here around the North and South Poles? Stowaway in the wide empty between worlds. What is wrong with me that I think these dark thoughts at a moment like this one? The baby wails, pumps oxygen frantically in and out. I concentrate on her face. The midwife wipes her clean. Fresh from my sister's spare room. Here. Our shul and apartments are so full of the missing, those who will never arrive, and yet here you are, a little girl who will make more Jews someday. How strange, how wondrous. Tateleh recites a blessing. I utter the Hebrew rapidly through my tears. Hannah moans. The midwife gives me a bottle of water and I hold it to my sister's mouth. "Touch her," she tells me. The baby's scalp quivers under my palm, like something inanimate coming to life.

According to our tradition, the child receives the names of relatives, but if she's named for a living relative, the angel of death may get confused and take the baby instead of the old person. Tateleh tells Hannah when I am not there (she tells me later, when he goes out for groceries) that he has been writing letters to his parents, brother and sisters for a year now and there has been no answer. He has never mentioned any letters to me. What does he think I would do? Crash to the floor wailing and beat it with my womanly fists? *Nu.* I may be only twenty-five, but I know what's what. People are people are people. I read the news. And, a strange thing I have never told anyone, that sometimes— no, often—when I look deeply into a person's eyes, I can tell what they're thinking. The sentences and motivations slide around under their gaze like a deck of cards being shuffled and reshuffled. People rarely surprise me. If you watch for long enough, they will reveal themselves. But my trick doesn't work on Louis. He is so easy, so light. So unlike the boys I grew up with, shouldering an unseen freight.

Louis does not even know how to pray. I have never met someone with nothing to hide.

Louis and Tateleh sit across from each other. Tateleh spreads butter on slices of black bread, asks me to bring the pot of tea from the kitchen. He is doing that thing where he takes too long with a simple task, in order to observe the person sitting across from him. Louis is pretzelled in his suit, trying not to look like a little boy. When they speak to each other, I am sharply aware of his Yiddish accent; it's so rare that I hear him speak English. English makes him sound hesitant, uneducated. Louis speaks rapidly, and I watch Tateleh's eyebrows swarm around his forehead, as he decodes and maps out his sentences. His world – home, shul, work, friends—is in Yiddish. He tells Louis, "Call me Izzy." A fake English name, silly-sounding, like a dog's name. Louis stares at Tateleh's yarmulke, and I can read his thoughts: he is wondering if he will ever have to wear one. Walk around with a sign that says JEW. No, I've always known that Louis won't convert. He wouldn't be accepted even if he tried—lanky like an adolescent deer, a tall standing wave of smooth hair, blue eyes, guilelessness. Tateleh leans forward and pushes a slice of bread into his mouth, chews slowly.

Louis says, "I'm very sorry about what's happening over there." The war is underway. When a young man at shul enlisted, Tateleh had shaken his head and scoffed, "Imagine, a Jew going there on purpose. Meshuga."

Tateleh chews for a long time, sips tea. "Happen before, happen again," he says. He shrugs. "*Tsuris.*" His word for everything.

After a while, Louis gives up and eats bread and drinks tea. I stand in the kitchen doorway. Tateleh asks me to bring in a plate of herring and crackers.

Louis asks me, "Do you have any cheese?"

Tateleh releases a low rumble. "No cheese with this," I say for him. Louis's eyes startle and stretch a bit; he recovers quickly. Tateleh shoves the plate toward him. "You have problem with me? Eat fish." He laughs. Louis looks down, places a cracker on his pink tongue.

After Louis leaves to walk home to his parents' house two neighbourhoods away, I sit across from Tateleh, reading the newspaper. Tateleh watches me.

"You shouldn't read so much about the war," he says. "It will make you sad."

I decide to ask him. "Did you hear from your brother?" His brother is younger than him, has a number of children.

"Nothing." He chews, his hazel eyes settling on me. "We will wait."

"But this seems different," I start to argue. "There are more countries—"

"*Nu?* Always we are blamed."

He slides a finger around his plate, exhausted from the encounter with Louis. He has asked me to not tell my friends about the engagement; to give him time to tell the people at shul first. He thinks that will make things easier on me.

"Is that why you left?"

He sighs. "First the army."

"The army?"

"Russian army. Every Jewish family had to give a boy."

"I didn't know you were in the army."

"A horrible thing, being a Jew in the Russian army."

"Oh."

"They kick me, they scream *Yid*, I fight for them."

"Oh."

"Then, pogroms. All the time, pogroms."

"Were you in a pogrom?"

He lifts his hands. "Of course! How not to be? They come to our villages, burn our houses, take our women. They hang my rabbi from a tree."

I stare at him, wordless. After a lifetime of silence, why is he telling me all of this now? I'm not ready.

"How many pogroms were you in?" I ask.

He lifts a hand and pulls it through the air in front of him. "One loooooooooong pogrom. Who can remember." He points at the newspaper. "Now yes, there is more. But always the same. People are people are people. People are *tsuris*."

"I know."

"Never trust, Charna. Never trust."

I nod.

"And now, Hannah has her baby. We start over. *Nu?*" He stares at me, eyes oddly glazed, the table vast between us. "Still, you want to marry him?"

I shrug.

He shakes his head. "Life is hard. Why make more problems."

I'm not like Hannah, devout and content with a husband who is stupider than her and never has a word to say, but wears the right kind of thing on his head.

"It will be hard for your children." He gets up to leave. "He's a nice boy, even if he's not a Jew. *Baruch hashem*."

Blessed.

SOMA

The ocean is blessed with boundless light as we emerge from the dark of the forest. Melanie tramps ahead of me. I'm relieved that the yahrzeit is over, as I am every year, that old feeling evaporating from my bones, temporary dark marrow. With this yahrzeit done, I'm the same age Grandma Charna was when the Holocaust was over. Maybe this will be the last year I will go through this during her yahrzeit. One day, my grief will be normal. The ocean sends blue emergency flares through spaces between the black branches. Melanie yells back at me, "Oh my god oh my god, wait till you see, it's so beautiful!" I study the ground ahead of me for roots, gigantic on this part of the coast, muscled arms reaching out of the earth. Melanie calls to me to hurry up. She read about this beach weeks ago while she was googling everywhere to go on the island; it's a medical-school dropout hangover, her love of detail. She's at the edge of the shining water, waving at me. How did I end up with someone like her? Someone easy, competent. From this beach we can see the whole channel, the dark edges of neighbouring islands mushrooming from the water, streaked black and white with atmosphere. As we walk along the edge of the ocean, Melanie points out the islands and names them. We walk for a long time, around a narrow point where the black rock juts out, crusted with oysters. The next beach is flooded with mist. Melanie shrieks softly and grabs my hand when three figures materialize several metres in front of us. The mist has made us distance-blind. A woman and two men stand on the sand, dressed formally in black suits and white dress shirts. The woman is holding a thick leather-bound book and one of the men holds a bottle of champagne.

"Hi," Melanie says.

The woman says, "I guess you aren't David and Derek."

"What?" Melanie says.

"Maybe we should get going," one of the men says.

"No, no, no. We need to wait a bit longer," the other man says. I notice their wingtip shoes, which the salt and sand will scar and ruin.

"It's been an hour."

"Sorry," Melanie says. "We're just on a walk."

"We're witnesses."

"Witnesses?"

The woman interrupts. "I'm a marriage commissioner."

"The couple is extremely late," one of the witnesses says.

"I bet Dave fucking bailed," the other witness says, and stares disconsolately at the ocean.

The marriage commissioner sighs. "This is rare, but it happens."

"How often?" one of the witnesses asks.

"I've been doing this five years and it's happened about eight times."

"Holy shit!"

"Not really. Better early than never."

"I suppose."

"How long can you wait?" Melanie says.

"It depends. An hour is normally my limit."

One of the witnesses grabs his phone from his pocket, releases a long moan. "They're not coming."

Melanie turns to me. "I think we should do it."

"What?"

"Can you marry us?"

The marriage commissioner stares. She's in her sixties; maybe this is her retirement project, to marry gay couples on remote windswept beaches.

She hesitates. "Technically, yes. All we need is two witnesses."

"Let's do it!"

"How long have you been together?" one of the witnesses says.

"Four years."

The other witnesses hold up the bottle of Veuve Clicquot. "I have booze," says one.

"Come on, babe," Melanie says to me. Her eyes glow with something manic close to transcendence. The witnesses in the background hold up their arms in excitement. "If we don't do it now, we never will."

CHARNA

We are married with few witnesses. Hannah comes with Joshua, who looks so tired. Louis's mother comes, but his father doesn't. Louis has shielded me from how unhappy his family is that he's marrying a Yid. I know why Tateleh isn't here—because no rabbi will officiate a marriage like this one. Some of Louis's friends from work are here, and some cousins and an uncle from out of town. No one from our shul is here. I thought I might feel brave and free today, but instead I feel I've eaten bad fish and am going to tip over. I've never been inside a church before. Louis's family isn't religious, but his mother has friends who come here, and the Protestant minister agreed. He shook my hand respectfully and patted my shoulder. I refuse to be a passive receptacle for anyone's pity. The English blessings are stiff, foreign, not the supple weave of Hebrew. I focus on Louis's face, his gentle features. We want to have a baby right away. I will name our child according to Ashkenazi tradition, I have decided, with my mother's initials. Louis has agreed. "We can do whatever we want," he's told me. I warned him what would happen, the wave of disapproval—silence—that would descend on me, the disappearance of all invitations, the women no longer greeting me in Yiddish in the street. A man in Tateleh's tea circle has stopped attending, sent a letter accusing Tateleh of allowing me to go against our people. I know, I know: with so many dead and dying, how could I leave? Zev Guttman embraced me and said, "We are still *mishpocheh*." It's not the same for Louis. The service is simple. Hannah yells, "Mazel tov." Louis's mother claps and claps and claps. Louis jumps up and down three times. We eat white cake with buttercream and fruit in the basement. Hannah gives me a box from Tateleh. In it is his book of Isaac Bashevis Singer stories and a gold-and-blue siddur in Hebrew. I open the cover and there is my name, Hannah's name, and our mother's name in faint cursive, with our Hebrew names in flawless script. He could not be here, so he sent her instead. Hannah takes the siddur from my hands. "Why didn't he give this to me when I was married?" she says competitively. "I didn't know he had this." I take the book back, hold it in my hands. I know why Tateleh has done this. This siddur came with them from their shtetl, their home. I think until the end that he will come to the reception, rush in, make a surprise appearance. He does not. He is at shul, or with his friends drinking tea, or out walking along the Red River.

Three families arrive in our shul from Czechoslovakia, smuggled out by relatives. Hannah repeats to us their stories from the women's prayer circle, of neighbours stripped naked in the street and herded onto a train. People going and no people coming back. Tateleh gets up from the table and leaves my apartment. "I don't want to listen to this." I think about the night he and Basha argued about the letters. I know from Hannah that the letter-writing circle has continued to convene, but I am no longer invited. I hold my belly, filling with our first child, read the newspaper, and worry and worry and worry.

What a horrible world we are trapped in. I ask myself, why are we here during this time? Maybe it's cruel, I tell Hannah, to bring a Jew into this world.

Soma

She chose to be cremated, against Jewish tradition, so that her ashes could be scattered in the same place as Grandpa Louis's. In her tradition, her body belonged to g-d and should be returned untouched; but for Grandma Charna, her body had changed hands over her lifetime. We gathered—her children, grandchildren, four great-grandchildren. I held her ashes and allowed them to run through the spaces between my fingers into the Pacific. My brother refused to touch the ashes, backed up, saying he was too afraid. That night I slept in a bed in a hotel room with my brother. I woke in the middle of the night and there was Charna. She was a grey entity, sailing swiftly through the air. On one side of my vision there was a grey rocky expanse; on the other, a green island. Grandma Charna flew back and forth, back and forth, whipping through the air, between the grey rock and the green island. She had her wry expression on her face and my ears filled with her high, choppy, unmistakable laughter. I woke sitting up on the hotel bed, the room shaken bright. There is always a choice, she was showing me. You can move between. I slipped downward, awakened in the morning, as if from a drugged sleep, head pounding, full of a pain like the ballooning weight of an infected tooth. I hadn't drunk water in days, my muscles moaned, grasping my bones. My breath powdery. I felt afraid to open my eyes. Then, when I did, just the faint electric hotel glow and my brother's voice shimmered blind starlight above me.

She followed me for years. Just when I'd think she was gone, she would come back, her face sharp as ever in my dreams, making herself known. Stowaway.

CHARNA

In spite of their tall, fair, pale father, my children are dark-haired with brooding eyes. My first, a girl, looks like Hannah, my second like Tateleh, born the year the war ends. A stocky, wailing spirit, a black broom of hair. As my son grows, the news comes. The first time I see photos of the strange skeleton people holding the wire at the border of the camp, I bend and retch between my shoes onto the grocery store's grey floor. It is more horrible than any of us could have conjured. There was so much rumour and speculation that when the truth does come, it is not true.

It is not. A fever dream. Tateleh does not speak of it and I do not bring it up. I have learned from him, it's best not to poke around where you're not welcome. After all, I'm not young anymore. He visits with bags of hamantaschen and holds the boy. No news has travelled here at all from eastern Ukraine. The newspaper humans are all chest bone and stripe, digit and eye socket. My second baby, born the year the war ended. I feed him dumplings cooked in schmaltz, I feed him cake, I feed him soup. I cannot let him out of my sight. When he goes with Hannah and her children to the store, I sit at the window and worry, worry, worry. I imagine him lying on the road, Hannah hit by a car. I imagine him staggering freely down the street, a woman in a coat lifting him and stealing him away. At shul we hear things that are not in the newspaper. A family burned alive in their home, doors blocked by their neighbours, a piano used as a barricade. One man who survived by living in the forest, in a hole. For *two years*. A fairy tale. Something a child makes up about a forest. Sometimes I think they are unlucky, my children, to have a mother who has heard so much *tsuris*, who cannot read a newspaper without feeling sick. No, they are lucky to have a mother who sees things as they are, who will never tell them lies. Who will never say what they want to hear. Who knows, there are only people and what we do to each other. The news worsens, spreads its deep glow east as my boy continues to learn to speak and walk. He will never know these things, this awfulness that won't stop chasing us, even an ocean away. A Russian tells Tateleh at shul that he travelled west across Ukraine and Poland and saw the razed villages. None left. Finished. Done. Tateleh sits on our deck and drinks tea, and then our wine, not kosher, for hours. Tells Louis to leave him be. He wants to be alone.

He was right all along. All those letters written were for nothing, written to no one. Canada did not care. I watch him through my kitchen window as I rinse and stack my yellow plates. His hat on his knees. What is he thinking? Is he thinking about the day he left? His shtetl a secret world buried between his ears. Shared with no one. Perhaps in bits, with his friends, in Yiddish. Never any word from his brother, and now?

Nu. Who can tell.

My boy, born in the year of the news of the dying, is playful and light as Louis. He floats easily between people. Sits on Tateleh's knee, shrieks with happiness. The eyelids, thick hoods; the hazel fields of their irises; the large hands sailing on the waves of laughter; and their shrugs, just the same, easy and heavy.

The borders are open now and the remnant drift into our streets, Tateleh's shul.

Hannah invites me again to her Hadassah gatherings at her apartment, and I scoop the herring into the Lazy Susan, heap crackers in the centre.

"*Sholem aleichem*, Charna," Basha says when she arrives.

I expect her snark but instead she asks how Tateleh is doing, and when I say, "Not well," she nods.

She says, "It is horrible, horrible. The Ukrainians were the worst, they say." Another woman nods. "The Ukrainians were the worst," she repeats, chewing.

How do they know this? How does anyone know anything, these days? Stories seep out of the cracks somehow.

"The Ukrainians, savages, they treated the Jews like dogs," Basha goes on.

113

She stares at me, waiting for a reaction. I stare blankly back at her. I have nothing to give her. We have no news. I am afraid to ask Tateleh now, to reawaken his grief. I remember the night in the kitchen when he told me about the pogroms, his rabbi hanged in a tree, his voice flinty and quiet. The few people who survived traded stories in the displaced persons camps, compared notes of disappeared places. Some of them have joined Tateleh's tea circle and perhaps he can ask what he needs to ask there. None of the women ask after Louis, but I understand why. You can only expect so much from people.

SOMA

Melanie won't talk to me during the ride back to the cabin. I drive and she gazes through the window, her chin tilted away, contained fury. She flings her bag down by the door, goes upstairs and climbs into bed. I take her iPhone out of her bag, input her passcode (her mother's birthday), and google "nazi" and "surrey" and "vancouver" and "canada." Last night there was a bomb threat at the Jewish Community Centre in Vancouver. The article says that children's aquatic classes and a concert were evacuated, police searched the building, and no bomb was found. There's a new ban on Muslims entering the States. Is this how it begins? I put her phone back in her bag.

I make two cups of tea and climb the stairs.

The quilt is pulled up over her head.

"I made tea," I say.

When I lie down beside her, she rolls away.

"I'm sorry," I say.

114

She emerges, tears and sweat. Her hair a deep and wild hive. "I can't believe you," she shouts hoarsely.

"Why do we need to be married?"

"I don't want to talk to you."

"It was just so—sudden."

We face each other. Her shoulders tremble.

"Everything doesn't have to be picked over for a thousand years," she spits.

The marriage commissioner and witnesses wandered off into the mist in subdued disappointment when it became clear that a spontaneous wedding wouldn't be happening.

"This whole trip was about your grandmother for you."

"I'm sorry."

"That prayer. Your whole family is like this."

How did she know about Kaddish?

"Why can't you just let yourself be happy?"

Curled on the couch downstairs, I check my email on her phone while she rests. There's a note from my father. He's forwarded me several articles about the bomb threats in Vancouver. He wants to know if I'm taking any classes at the Jewish Community Centre anytime soon. I want to write back to him, these people are nuts, extremists. A radical fringe group in their brief heyday. It will die down, soon, give it time. But I know not to reply. An update on the trip would only set off a fresh cascade of worries. Did you see a doctor about your leg? Do you have Tylenol? How are you sleeping? And eating? When will you be back where I can see you?

CHARNA

I go with Tateleh to Shabbat to pay my respects for Zev
Guttman. It is my first time back in shul since I married
Louis. There is talk about Zev's suicide—it is against G-d
to take one's own life. Can we know what is against G-d?
Perhaps blind obedience is the worst sin of them all. Zev's
sister and her family were on that ship turned back in the
Pacific when this whole nasty mess was starting. Every
member of his family perished in camps. He sent money,
wrote letters. Zev Guttman, a prominent lawyer, he could
do nothing. "A waste of life," Tateleh says to me, furiously.
"A waste of life. They should hang William Lyon Mackenzie
King in the street." People came here believing they would
get established, then bring their families over, only to look
over their shoulders and see their footsteps disappearing
behind them. A cruel joke played by G-d. The shul is exactly
the way I remember. Siddurs piled on a table at the door.
Dust, paper, sweat. Every childhood Saturday. I feel people staring at me; I will always be the woman who turned
her back, not quite a shiksa, but something in between, a
hybrid, not to be trusted. But I don't care about them—I
am here for Zev, who always said hello to me in the street
after I married Louis unlike the yentes who snubbed me,
Zev who came to Tateleh's tea circles every week during
the years of endless *tsuris*. I have often wondered how the
men of Tateleh's generation, the ones who came alone and
learned their worlds evaporated behind them, could bear
it. To be left behind, to go without, to never know. How
could they say Kaddish for so many dead, for those who
vanished in great groups? This prayer has always been the
one that reaches for something underneath my doubt. The

116

prayer I have missed, felt its weekly absence. Our prayer of mourning, yet it makes no mention of mourning, is only a sustained praise of G-d. The prayer we recite to ease the transfer of a soul from one world to another. After death, there are still things we need. I have said this prayer in unison with Tateleh innumerable times over my lifetime. When he is gone, I will say these words for him. We repeat and repeat and repeat as the beloved travels farther away through time, until they are the shape of our voice. Only life upon all of us. When I am gone, who will say Kaddish for me? Only the wry laughter of my children, named for our beloveds from the other world. Mighty be the name. Only the praise and the consolation. Only the beauty of creation, beyond blessing and song.

SOMA

The ferry crossing is a single rotation of a crystal glass.

We don't speak.

I go upstairs on my own. Melanie stays on the car deck, scrolling through her iPhone, a magic portal I am not permitted to access.

I browse the magazines and drink hot chocolate, leaning against the window. Children press themselves to the windows at the front and search the Pacific for non-existent whales. *They're all dead,* I want to tell them. *Or have consumed so much pollution that they may as well be mobile nuclear reactors, roaming the ocean.* I laugh, and a kid stares at me.

"What's so funny?" the kid says.

"Nothing," I say.

"You're sitting by *yourself laughing*?" he says.

"Crazy lady," I hear him mutter as I walk away.

Fuck you, you damn kid.

When I get into the car, the radio is pumping country hits, and Melanie turns and holds up her phone. "I got an email from your dad."

"Yeah?"

"He wants to know if you're okay. Did you tell him what happened on the beach?"

"No, of course not."

"Really?"

"Yes. Really."

She exhales. "Okay."

"What did his email say?"

"Oh, the usual. I hope you guys are having a good time. Lots of dolphin emoticons. Wants us to come over for dinner next week. You know, seven times."

"I didn't tell him anything."

"Yeah, I thought I might just write back, 'Thanks for your note, your daughter spent our trip in mourning, inexplicably injured her leg, disappeared in the middle of the night for a mysterious expedition, and humiliated me on the beach in front of total strangers after I made a spontaneous declaration of love.'" She puts her phone into her pocket. "'Wish you were here.'"

"There aren't enough dolphin emoticons for that one."

We watch passengers return to their cars.

I point out the kid from upstairs. "That kid was an asshole to me."

"What?"

"He called me a crazy lady."

"Why?"

"They were all looking for whales, and I was thinking about telling them that all the whales are probably dead and then I started to laugh."

"I've explained to you before that other people can't hear your thoughts."

"Their loss."

I take the sandwiches out of the glove compartment and pass one to her.

"Does your dad know?" she says, chewing.

"Know what?"

"The stuff about your grandma."

"What do you mean?"

"You know. How once a year, on her death-iversary, you act like you're losing your mind."

I chew. "After we scattered her ashes, I told him I saw her cross over, and he didn't seem surprised."

I feel her eyes on my cheek, like the heat of a strong light. "Really?" She waits. "Did he say anything?"

"Yeah, he said, he waited for her to come to him, and she didn't."

We listen to car motors cough awake one by one, the ocean groan and roll its head against the ship.

"That's really sad," she says finally, chewing.

"It's not sad. It's just how we are."

She breaks pieces of her sandwich off with her fingers, eats them one by one.

"I feel bad for your dad."

"Why?"

"Stuck in the middle."

I remember how, once during undergrad, when I'd emailed my father records I'd found of our relatives who'd been killed, he'd called me up and said, "Why do you need to be a gravedigger?" *Does that make you a grave?* I'd thought, bitterly.

"I'm sorry about this weekend," I say. "All of it. It was awful."

"What about now?" Melanie asks.

"She's gone now," I say. "I can tell. It's over."

"Are you just saying that to make me happy?"

I look at her. Her eyes large, questioning.

"It's the truth."

"How can we tell?"

I want a Jewish wedding, I tell her. I want to invite people and feed them. I just want it to be normal. Yes, she says. I just need more time, I say.

I always need more time.

What if I run out?

Wait, and there's nothing?

I've missed my chance?

There will never be enough.

Always best to save some for later.

She knows me too well to be reassured. She places her hand beside mine on the steering wheel and for a moment, I swerve.

Charna

I have often thought, how could something like that take only a handful of years? The longer I live, the more I think about it. My head hurts to think about it so much. Years after the war was over, I finally asked Tateleh, did he ever get word from anyone. He held his hands up apart from each other in a shell. No one. My boy asks me where we are from. A natural question, but very annoying. The question does something to me, makes an animal curl at the base of my spine. I tell him, you were born here. If you want proof, I have the proof in the stretch marks. You don't believe me? *Nu?* You don't believe me? Go off, then. See how far that gets you. I won't give you a pretty story with a coat of fresh paint. See where it gets you, to go looking around there in all that mess. Walk yourself backwards off a cliff, see how it goes. Flat on your back, looking at the stars. What did you expect. A miracle? No, this isn't something you read in a book. This is real history. You'll just get yourself all worked up, thinking about these things. You can think and think and think and have nothing to show for it. People. Sometimes, there is nothing to understand. Listen to your mother. Anyway, it's years ago now, who can remember. The people I know who lived through it don't even like to talk about it, and so who am I to bother them? So. You leave people to their memories. The past takes care of itself if you let it, settles down on its own. The rest doesn't matter. It doesn't need to be so complicated. People make things complicated with all this thinking and thinking, but actually things are very simple. There's nothing for you there, only sadness. Where are you from? Like the goys say—immaculate conception. I named you for my mother, may her memory be for a blessing. Her name is written into yours. I wanted you and I made you. We are here and that is all there is. And, in any case, I forget. The Black Sea is all I remember, and the rest, who knows. The Ukrainians were the worst. That I know. Murderers, all of them. They tried to get rid of us.

Your grandfather didn't like to talk about these things, and I suppose I got it from him. The not talking. He didn't like to talk about where he was from. You don't need to be a genius to understand why. Just look around you. You still want to bother me with your questions? Life is long, but not long enough to understand the things that happened over there. The things I heard, you wouldn't believe, you wouldn't want to know. The things people do to people. If I told you the things I heard, you would never forgive me. Your ears would fall off your head. When you have children, they will never need to worry about any of these meshuga things. All this. Best to leave it behind. For what, do you want to know? Things happen. Horrible things, normal things. And so? Who can tell the difference sometimes. People are people are people. Why do you want to upset me? Listen to me. You can be different. You don't need to go rummaging around. There's nothing there for you. You were always a happy boy. Only listen to me when I say, nothing good will come of digging up what is already done. It's in the past now. It's done. Don't come around with your questions. Only sit with me. Only sit at my table and eat my food. Never leave me.

Self-Help Liturgy

S H O R T

And that's when Kendra gets up on the table and announces she has a game for us all to play.

"The name of the game is Is Life Long or Short!" she shouts like a kindergarten teacher directing a field trip. Someone baboon-hoots disconsolately from one of her sagging wing chairs, jammed into a corner to make room for all the grief pooling in the centre of the carpet.

"Get down, Kendra!" someone yells.

I don't recognize the voice but something in me rallies to their request. *Get down*. Looking up at her is viscerally tiring to my eyes. My new glasses feel heavy, pressing my forehead back as I look up at her, her arms raised like a prophet's. "The game goes like, everyone says whether they think life is long or short and why," she continues to holler.

The same person yells, "This isn't funny, Kendra!"

Someone else says, "That isn't even a game. Games don't have one rule."

A bunch of people murmur in agreement. Laughter.

"Nononononononono!" Kendra says. I've played this game before and it's really fun!" Kendra is the kind of person who would wear a Wu-Tang Clan crop top to a funeral to honour the deceased's musical preferences.

I feel sorry for her. She's losing control of the crowd. So I stand up.

I sway. I've been drinking all afternoon, since before the church thing, and the group sad-shuffle-dances over to Kendra's place and throughout the extended rotation of Chinese takeout and freezer sausage rolls and SuperValu baked brie with canned cranberry sauce tipped on top, Hallowe'en costume gore.

I hear my voice soar outside of myself: "Short."

Kendra's eyes flare on me. I'm normally pretty quiet in a crowd.

"Thanks, Soma! Uh. Why?"

I can see that she didn't really expect anybody to answer.

Faces turn to me. I know most of these people, but haven't seen a lot of them in years. My mind reels back to camping trips as a kid, flat on my black, watching the stars until I lost consciousness. All of their wide-open, observing faces. At rest, ready for someone to speak. Cognac paddles sloppily through my blood looking for somewhere firm to throw a rope. We're all here for Elijah, and so it's time for me to speak.

I say, "Because. Look at this. Look at it. It's over for Elijah. Short. It's short. It's short."

You're so drunk, Soma, sit down, the fierce, anxious twin inside me whispers. Faces slope and couple, the starlight from my eyes rippling over them. A grumble of agreement rises under my boots. I really need to buy new boots. These ones have long narrow cracks in the rain-tarred leather, right foot still icy. This season in Vancouver when nothing ever gets dry. Bog city. Tidal pools in the gutters, water always wearing down the cement, coming up through the cracks in everything. I hate this party and wanted to leave hours ago. Why did I even come? Knew staggering down the chipped concrete path to Kendra's side entrance that it was a point-of-no-return moment, mind galloping ahead to texting my brother drunkenly hours from now, avoiding his replies, sleeping bent between couch cushions, hangover backache, the internal bruising of chosen mistakes. I tried to kick off my wet boots and could not get free, so I stayed on the couch and here I still am. I've been here for years.

I stand up and the faces are upturned, waiting.

Slow-clap of the freezer door opening and closing, bottles dragged off hook-toothed ice.

"So your answer is, it's short." She nods at me, trying to get me to sit down.

"This is an exorcism!" I scream. My arms out, holding the room steady. Kendra takes a step backward.

"Thanks for sharing, Soma."

"Long or short! Yeah!" someone hoots.

LONG

Right now somebody is talking about that moment, I tell Jim three days later. That moment when I screamed the word *exorcism* like a fucking maniac. Right this instant, somebody is talking about that.

He unfolds his hands, skin like waxed Pink Lady apples. "And what would they be saying?"

"That I'm..." I search my mind, full of faces. "Crazy."

"Crazy people are sometimes correct."

"That's not the point."

Jim shrugs. "Then why worry about it?" He holds his lit cigarette out the window.

"Because I care."

"Could you care less?"

"No."

He laughs. "Then care some more."

"Fuck off."

"You paid for my cappuccino," he says. "It's your time to waste."

Around us in the dim coffee shop that occupies that first floor of our apartment building, students pound away on MacBooks. We've been coming here a couple times a week since we met while moving into neighbouring apartments two years ago. The first time I saw Jim I wondered what had happened in his life that someone as old as him was renting a tiny apartment identical to mine. His shoes were too beautiful to belong to my neighbour. Wingtips with tiny white holes bored in the leather.

His high laughter circles my ears as I hold my forehead against the tabletop. Then he drums his fingers on its edge. "Soma. You do this to yourself."

"No. Something has happened."

"Something has happened?"

"Something has happened."

"What has happened?"

"A death."

"A death has happened."

"Yes."

"Yes. A death has happened," he repeats. "You didn't tell me everybody was talking about Elijah's death. You told me everybody was talking about you and the drinking game."

"It wasn't a drinking game."

"No?"

"No, it was a game *while* drinking."

"Well. There are games we are more prone to play while intoxicated."

"A drinking game is a game where drinking is part of the rules."

"No. According to you and your sophomoric friends, that's a memorial."

LONG

I got the event notification a week before the memorial/party and clicked "Maybe Attending" so that I could keep an eye on it. It would just stress me out, getting notifications needling at me to make a decision. Those tiny red numbers follow me around like a swarm of insects. So I have this system to pre-manage events as they approach. Deleting the invitation for Elijah's memorial party (after the brief church thing) would make me feel too guilty—what kind of person avoids a memorial on Facebook? Also the way Kendra wrote the event description—*hey guys so a bunch of us have been talking about how to support us all in remembering Elijah and my place is pretty central so I'm just going to bake some brie (yay Costco! lol) and put out some bread and you guys can bring whatever else you want to eat, this is nothing formal and everyones welcome bring your partners and drinking is allowed BYOB but no blacking out at my place I'm way too old for that shit*—and on and on like that. *To support us all in remembering Elijah*—the way we'd swallowed that language, pasted it onto a person we actually knew, like a self-help liturgy. And, worst of all, pasting it onto Elijah,

who would have rolled his eyes, hissed, "Bitch, please."
Master of self-improvement. People started posting on the
event page right away, about being out of town, about Elijah, and photos of Elijah from our years in undergrad where
we met and his scattered shitty jobs, one of Elijah naked on
Wreck Beach being held aloft by three skinny guys, and one
guy thanked Kendra for "taking one for the team." A photo
of Elijah flipping burgers at Wendy's. A photo of Elijah lying
face down on a sunny lawn, arms out. I've known Kendra
since I was eighteen. Salt of the earth. When you die, she
will put brie in the oven and put out the piles of empties
the next morning and send condolence cards to your family
who she's never met in person, your family you swore you'd
never go back to, the ones you never stopped running from.

SHORT

Elijah's problem was that he had no filters.

The problem with hanging around with people with no
filters is that you have two options: listen to all their unfil-
tered crap, or become the filter.

Being someone's filter—that shit is exhausting.

I can't be your friend if it's too hard to listen to what
you're saying. I don't mean this is too hard for me right
now, but physically I can't do this with my body right now.
If I listen to you for one more minute, I will start to bleed
from my eyeballs.

It isn't fair to say these things after the fact, but here we
all are.

Sometimes you just have to tone it down for the sake of
people around you. You know?

My strongest memory of Elijah, for no particular reason:

We are sitting on the filthy concrete steps that go down into the basement of a building on campus. We've been drinking all afternoon and he starts pulling at his clothes, repeating, "What is this? What is this?" and I don't know what to do, so I sit there naming things for him: "That's a sweater, those are pants." I forget the rest of what happened.

These are your pants, this is your sweater—you can say these things a thousand times to a person, but it will never be enough, if you're just the filter, waving your fingers in front of their eyes while they look at the sun.

Drop your hands. Proceed calmly.

LONG

After I yell the thing about the exorcism, Kendra's Is Life Long or Short game fizzles out. We all know where Elijah came from, and I sit there like a human bad joke. My cheeks roast, and I think, you assholes, I did more for him than any of you even tried to. She gives me a look, like I've ruined things for her. I stare back at her, telegraphing: you tried to turn around a memorial with a drinking game about life and death—I don't think I'm the problem here. At the same moment, we both look away.

I sit for a long time beside a guy who smells like an old fridge with its door left hanging open. He talks unprompted about his thesis writer's block for a long time. What is it about PhD students and their Stockholm syndrome? After he's switched conversation topics to the intimacy problems in his long-distance relationship, someone sitting on the couch across from us drinking straight from a pot-bellied bottle of Chianti says, "How long have you known each other?" and when I answer, "We just met," the other person starts to laugh, then cry, and I get up and walk to the other side of the room. Too much crying over in that corner near the Chianti.

Kendra confronts me in the kitchen. "An exorcism?" she hisses. "How are you *holding up*?" The way she says "holding up" means "you are a liability."

"I don't need a babysitter," I snap back, my mind skipping ahead, loosened by alcohol.

"I don't want this to get messy," Kendra says.

"Is life long or short?" I half-yell. It is hard to get undrunk, in the moment. And then, "Oh my god, did you just *shove* me?"

"I didn't shove you, just don't be weird tonight." She takes her hands off my shoulders.

We stand, staring at each other, and she gathers me into her arms.

I can tell she cleaned her apartment for Elijah. She smells like Comet cleaner and brie grease. She's wearing a maroon dress with a clashing purple scarf because she doesn't own any black clothes. Had her hair done. Holding her, I feel the years of our friendship. The friendships of my twenties have been a series of misfires and explosions, but Kendra has endured, indifferent to the deep pendulum rhythm of my moods. When her mother died two years back, she called me and I drove her to the small town in northern BC where she was from, called in sick to my job at the restaurant, spent three days taking her around the town, finding a coroner, sitting with her relatives, washing and folding her mother's bras and chunky sweaters in the laundromat below the movie theatre. Her uncles brought buckets of KFC to her mom's place and we ate in a circle on the living room couches. We slept in the same bed and I wanted to take home every too-thin dog I saw at the side of the road. A van parked behind the church was where people got dental checkups. The town she's from is bisected by a highway and neighboured by a hydroelectric dam, but none of her relatives talked about their jobs. Her mom's memorial was in a tiny proper funeral home that was like a cross between an IHOP and a bingo hall. I drove us back down to Vancouver and we both went back to our jobs the next morning as if nothing had happened. She sent me a text message: *eating sushi bad rnb playing after were dead bruno mars will keep playing in sushi places.*

She holds me now and rubs my back in wide, soft circles.

Walking away, she says over her shoulder, "Try not to be like him tonight."

Long

About a week after the party, Jim knocks on my door with a bag of doughnuts and two Americanos. He steps over the clothes and books covering the floor of my apartment and puts the cups down on the windowsill.

"Jim, is life long or short?" I ask.

He drinks. "I don't want to answer that question."

"You have to answer!"

"Why?"

"Because you're the only old person I'm friends with."

He laughs softly and holds his palm against the window.

"There's nothing to understand, Soma."

"What do you mean?"

"No doctor will tell you this, but depression is a terminal illness."

Outside, wind sucks meat from the bones of the bare trees.

When my eyes return to his face, he's blowing hot white circles on the glass. "You should clean your windows, Soma."

"Whatever."

"Seriously. It's disgusting in here. You're a disgusting pig."

Jim's apartment next door is austerely clean: two pine bookcases full of alphabetized records and a low marble slab table holding up glazed turquoise bowls full of glass fishing floats. Over the course of my many visits there, the door to the bedroom has never been left open. It's possible he sleeps on a wooden plank like a penitent gay monk. After he got the payout from the government for his botched transfusion, he did a "radical downsize" and decided to live out his fatigue as simply as possible.

"I'm too tired," I tell him.

"You might feel better if you weren't sitting here festering like an old bag." He blows more circles on the window, the steam matching the white of his dense stubble. "Come, Soma," he says, and I follow him around my tiny apartment, sorting clothes into piles and loading stray plates and cups into the sink. When we're finished we go next door to his apartment and he boils noodles and stirs them with eggs and ham. We drink glasses of white wine and then green tea, and I fall asleep on his couch before he leaves for his mid-afternoon walk. I dream about Elijah running through an empty field, legs cycling as he tumbles

through space, the burnt summer grass glowing and bris-
tling behind him.

Short

The strangest thing about Elijah's memorial party is that
he's here. The way he holds his glass—limp, loose, like
he's about to let it slip and go crashing down. He always
finds a wall to stand beside and he holds his glass just this
way. Sometimes, looking at him, I can tell he's forgotten
where he is. Here, where he's surrounded by people, a veil
comes over him, a quietness between him and everyone
else. When people speak to him and he's unplugged, he
smiles with fond disinterest. Everybody should stop trying
so hard, that smile says to me. It's such a shame we have
to try so hard with each other. I remember feeling that way
when I was seventeen, nineteen, a sense that it was all a
charade, we were all just going through the motions of becoming humans. It takes a while to grow a person. But at
some point, we all outgrow that charade feeling, don't we?
Or pretend to. But you can tell Elijah never lost it—you can
see it on him. He wears it. It makes people wary. He isn't
the kind of person you can say that to, though.

We hadn't talked in a few weeks when I heard the news. I
would never say this out loud, but when I heard he jumped
from the Lion's Gate Bridge I wasn't surprised. Kendra
called me to break the news. I couldn't have predicted. A
part of me knew that he wasn't in it for the long haul. He
looked at all of us as if we were optional.

I can't tell you the colour of his eyes. I think of him, hold
him right here in my mind, and I think of his watchfulness,

133

a gaze with no colour. Light laid on shallow water. Barely perceptible movement. Just passing through.

At his party, I watch him. He witnesses the whole thing. He's there, standing in the corner, in the shelter of the wall, watching all the people he's known over the course of his twenties drain the black and copper bottles that crowd the counters and tables. Bored, he watches me fade in and out of a dozen conversations with people I've forgotten, people who knew me only as Elijah's friend, the one people always assumed would pick Elijah up from the hospital when things got sketchy and he dropped out of the world for periods of time. He watches me drink and drink and drink, argue with Kendra, he watches the young men in black suits from his home arrive and reduce the room to silence, he still hates them, but all our bodies together in the same room praying and drinking, there is something in that worth hanging around for, and he watches me go home with a woman at dawn.

Long

At some point in the ageless pale hours of early morning, someone reprises the game. The leader is a friend of Elijah's from the comic-book festival he worked at for two summers. Misha, with a stop-start way of speaking, a head of red leaves. They fucked for a while, on and off. Elijah cared less. The top and bottom buttons of his shiny purple dress shirt undone. Elijah had a talent for collecting people. One time I told him he was the most non-judgmental person I'd ever known. He looked at me archly and answered, "It isn't that I don't judge, it's that I don't *care*."

He looked disappointed in me, as if I'd missed some very obvious point.

Misha raises his glass. "Long," he says.

Kendra, still moderating through the monocle of an amber glass: "Why long?"

Misha sweeps an arm out, as if clearing a great, invisible, cluttered table. "I'm thirty-three. I could live to be one hundred. That means I've lived one third of my life."

"Solid math." I turn and look for Elijah, but he isn't there; just some guy eating a slice of green quiche off his left knee.

"One third and think about it—how much of the first ten years do you remember? This is the part of our lives we'll remember all of. All of it."

"What a horrifying thought." Elijah?

"I mean, when you really think about it"—two sets of arms and legs in the corner unfurl from each other—"your twenties are just, like, preparation, getting ready. I mean"—most people are listening to him now, or too drunk to resist—"I mean, who here owns anything? Not a car. That doesn't count." I don't own a car. "Who has a kid? We are a *fucked generation*. None of us will ever own anything."

True—the recession set in the year I finished undergrad, and the economy won't change anything soon. The damage has been done. We'll live in tents like our ancestors. I pour water into my whisky.

"Misha..." Kendra's voice drifts up nervously.

"I'm not saying he was right."

"Misha, thanks. Game's over." Kendra scans the room nervously—she doesn't want this mess to dishonour his memory.

"I'm not saying that. I'm saying, I'm saying life is long because there's always more time. A lot more."

A few people applaud as Misha staggers a bit, raises both his arms.

"It's your Jesus year," Kendra says.

"What?"

"Thirty-three. Your Jesus year."

Misha laughs. "I'm Jewish."

"So was Jesus," I mumble.

"Isn't the whole point of Jesus that every year is your Jesus year?" A girl in the corner stares at us, her eyes conjoined in angry focus. No matter where you are and what you're doing, someone will be mad if you bring up Jesus.

"I don't know."

Misha points at Kendra. "What happens in your Jesus year?"

"Realization."

Misha points at me. "My child," he says. "Life is short."

Elijah was a year older than me. He was twenty-one the first time he got really sick. I visited him in the hospital. I remember very little of that visit. The white noise from the hidden machinery in neighbouring rooms irradiated the ventricles of the afternoons I spent there. His father hunched in the area for families, seafoam-green upholstered benches jammed together, and a rubber plant with a Santa hat on one branch. Elijah mumbled to me about the ocean, how it was full of people. He wanted me to understand that water is made of people, and that he had swum with them. That is why there is so much water, because that's where all the people go. Past and future people, he told me. We're all in there. I promised him that I understood, so that he would let me leave. His father only came that first time. They'd been back in touch for just a few years at that point.

"Jesus year—is that like the fundamentalist version of Saturn's return?" Misha says.

"It's different," Kendra says. I always forget she was raised Catholic. Somewhere in her is a streak of do-the-right-thing conservatism, the yellow stripe down the middle of the highway that bisects her hometown.

Someone I don't recognize pipes up helpfully: "I read a thing on Facebook recently that horoscopes are really popular with millennials because we have nothing stable to live for anymore."

"That's a reason to live, Soma," Misha says to me. "Your Jesus year."

Kendra steps forward, surprises me with her burst of anger. She's getting tired, wants everyone out of her place. "Soma," she says, "has many reasons to live."

SHORT

A girl I recognize, sort of, from university—we had a couple classes together probably, or maybe I just knew her from parties—turns to me at some point in the kitchen and says, "The skyline is ruined for me now."

"What?" I say.

"The view of the bridge. It's ruined now. I mean, I know that's selfish, but it's true. It was my favourite view in the city. That bridge is on every Vancouver postcard."

LONG

Outside, in the faint rain, a small cluster of bodies in the sweet smoke, a bit rancid, a bit potpourri. "Ah, cloves," someone says, and laughter is passed from hand to hand, pressed between wet burning fingers. Water seeps into the cracks in my boots again. Illuminated eyes float like bathyspheres. My mind plummets into a familiar well. The smoke does its old familiar work on me.

"—and when his dad stood up and said that stuff about compassion—fucking hypocrite—"

"—yeah—like, everyone knows, man—"

"—only came here once or twice—not that far—prairies—"

"—the whole time—so sick—Elijah—"

"—sorry your kid's a faggot—and you—"

"—that whole thing—"

"—Elijah would have hated—"

My skull aches, stretches, sections of bone drift and reassemble. Smoke enters and leaves, enters and leaves.

"—good to get some air—"

"—this is good stuff—"

"—things were chill until Kendra brought it down—"

"—that fucking game—"

Laughter.

"—fucking heavy—"

I watch a cloud of smoke take the form of a white fish and soar across the empty circle and into the night. Elijah was right about a lot of things.

"—fuck this—"

"—sweet guy—"

"—sweetheart—"

"—fucking waste—"

"—not a mean bone in—"

Inside, a restrained roar. The party is kicking into its third life. People who went home or out to eat or to spend time alone after the church service have circled back. Kendra told me she invited some guys from Elijah's hometown over for lemonade and coffee cake at the reception. "You invited *them?*" I'd asked her, disbelieving. Now, four tall guys in black suit jackets, white shirts, like an amateur Beatles cover band, are coming down the path. Hair combed to the side, eyes sober. Leering at them, I feel like a hyena caught in headlights on the side of the road.

"Is this the thing for Elijah?" one of them asks, a guy with a hawkish nose, hands pushed deep into his pockets. Once, I asked Elijah about his friends from where he grew up. He blew smoke smoothly: *Who cares? Robots.*

A broken circle of coughs. "Yeah."

They go inside. We drift in a lung of smoke. Rain shatters around the outside of my skull. Phantom touch of judgment says, *Don't smoke more.* It's a heavy wheel turning, slumping forward, completing a final turn into stillness, a silence that presses all the way down, into the floor of my mind. More, more, more. Elijah lying next to me on his bed, a cloud of our shared smoke drifting around us. Staring at the ceiling, he tells me about the Greyhound station in the middle of nowhere where he first cruised for men. The blue light in the tiny bathroom to make it harder for people to shoot up. He left young, but not young enough. His silence when I answer, "I slept outside when I was young too." When he says nothing, I turn my head and check to see if he's fallen asleep. His eyes are closed and smoke passes in and out of his mouth. His eyelids flutter. "Tell me the story," he says. Instead I tell him about how when I was in elementary school I got obsessed with a lamp that was supposed to treat seasonal depression, how I stole another girl's dad's credit card, a girl I had a crush on but didn't know what that was yet, a girl so mean-eyed and aloof I loved her for it, and I thought the lamp would cure my mother's *severe chronic mental illness*—here Elijah squeezes his eyelids shut, his mouth tenses into a rippling seam of restrained laughter—and then the girl and her friends jumped me in the hallway, and then when the lamp arrived it was a *piece of shit*, a blue glass light bulb in a white blobby stand like a knock-off Lego starship, and I knew it was a fake, I knew it like I knew the second I slipped that credit card out of that girl's back pocket that I was gay, but I used the lamp anyway, I coveted it, I prayed over it. I was too ashamed to show it to my father or even to Josiah, I kept that lamp to myself and I would turn it on and sit in front of it for hours at night, bathing in its cold, sugary radiance.

"How poignant," Elijah says, and we lie on our backs and laugh, push smoke from our empty pipes and watch it invent shapes against the ceiling and window, we laugh at all the creatures we have been and the weird joy of telling it to each other.

SHORT

I sit in Jim's kitchen and watch him heat the small iron pan he reserves for omelettes, melt butter, whisk eggs.

I can't stop thinking about the moment I leaped up and shouted that the party was an exorcism, I tell him.

Jim swivels and points his whisk at me. "Stop obsessing."

"I can't stop thinking about it," I groan.

It's been over a week since the party. I've ignored Kendra's messages. For a couple days after the party, people posted on the event page. More photos; sentimental shards of text. A meaningless social networking emotive mosaic. I've watched Kendra comment "Thank you!" on each one. She's made herself the page's only administrator, the moderator of memories of Elijah.

Jim asks me what I'm thinking about. I watch his face as I recite the story Elijah told me about when he ran away. Jim listens, his face relaxed, and then shakes his head. "Every queer gets thrown out sometime," he says.

SHORT

Kendra's living room is silent when I go back in. The guys in suits are at the centre, the tallest one muttering, hands pressed together. Kendra leans against the fridge, cheeks unnaturally white.

Misha lies on the couch, eyeing the smouldering end of his cigarette. "E.T., call home," he says, holding his finger a hair's breadth from the orange tip.

I scan the room. Most people are deep in prayer.

There was the brief service at the church Elijah had gone to on and off for the last couple years, but before that there had been another ceremony, back in Elijah's hometown, to which we, his second family, weren't invited. I wonder what they did with his soul, and if he can tell. Elijah's oldest sister had called me to stiffly relay her condolences; she would not be travelling. Is it the suicide or the gayness, I'd wanted to ask. This is why Elijah had no filters. They had been burned away. His leaving; his missing cells.

In the hospital, the third or fourth time, the psychiatrist sits across from me in the shoebox-sized room, her knees nearly touching mine, apologizes for the lack of space, the lack of time, writes continuously on her clipboard without looking up while I speak, as if transcribing the lyrics of a song as it plays, mutters occasional words to match mine—"filters," "self-help," "university." Elijah's presentation, she tells me, supports... And my brain downshifts into a mode between delirious bemusement and dark fatigue. "Presentation," I repeat. His presentation about what? My mind fumbles the handfuls of details to summarize Elijah, make her understand.

His psychosis, she tells me, has a strong storytelling element. She asks how I know Elijah, how did I come to be the one who brings him in when he's sick. I gaze at her listlessly. "He calls me," I say. "We met at school." The psychiatrist watches me, and puts the cap back on her pen.

"Where's his family?" she says.

"Have you checked the ocean?" I say, trying to be Elijah.

SHORT

It starts with self-help books. I drop by his place on a Tuesday. He's renting the back bedroom in an apartment with three other guys. We smoke weed on his windowsill. He points at each of the twenty-five or thirty books assembled in an arching rigid pattern on his bed, like the bones of a church window. Typical Elijah, gushing eagerly, ferociously, about his latest self-improvement project. Before this, there's been jogging, weightlifting, learning German on an app. He jumps forward onto the bed and tosses one of the books back to me, *The Highly Sensitive Person*. The cover has swoopy letters like a cookbook from the seventies. He's been going about things all wrong, he tells me. He needs to get to the root causes. All this time he's just been trying to fix the things he does, the things on the surface. "Bullshit!" he tells me triumphantly. So sure of himself, this time. I nod and nod. My head bobs numbly, an empty can on a riptide. When he had told me the story about running away after the conversion ceremony and I had told him the story about the lamp and the rest of the stories about my mother, everything, everything, something had happened, we had become family. "Now that I know," he says to me, sweeping an arm over the books, "I can do something about it," and then he repeats, "Now that I know, now that I know, now that I know." How intensely he wants me to know what he knows. He hands me one book, and another, and another, always sliding the books on the bed around, never leaves a gap. He's always read so much—recycled courses through a long series of majors—philosophy, history, political science, communication studies, then the attenuated fade into interdisciplinary studies, to try to cobble all those credits into something. Something to show for himself. When I graduated with a boilerplate literature degree, I didn't think about why Elijah wasn't graduating, even though he was older than me—he was already separate from the rest of us. Then we quickly became the same in how frequently we changed jobs, our frenetic aimlessness. The first few kitchens I worked in, I only lasted a few months. I only cared about the paycheque, to make rent, have my small space away from my brother and father for the first time.

Elijah hopped workplaces at a similar pace, but the reasons were always vague—a co-worker he suspected of stealing his phone; a manager who was reading his email. It was just the way he was. Sensitive, always having a hard time, taking everything to heart. "You can see my organs under the right light," he joked once. During one of his last jobs, at a shoe store, he'd CC'd me on a long email to a boss and co-workers. I skimmed the email, dull panic stirring in me, and deleted it when I got to the long, numbered list of grievances. One of the final items was a rambling critique of the manager's dog, in which Elijah catalogued the resemblances between the manager and his dog. THE DOG WHO CHOOSES THE HUMAN, Elijah wrote, REVEALS THE MARROW OF CHARACTER. DOGS SEE IN BLACK AND WHITE. At least there wasn't a diagram.

The books are helping, he tells me.

When he looks into my eyes, I feel abruptly shy, old fear runs aground on the floor of my stomach.

"This could help you too, Soma," he says. "We're the same, you know we are."

Now, since he flew from the bridge into the black dream at the edge of the city, my secrets are in the Pacific, dispersing like a suitcase of stars pushed overboard.

SHORT

Kendra sits between two of the guys from Elijah's home.

"What was Elijah like when he was young?" she asks.

I've never tried to picture Elijah as a kid and now when I try for the first time, I can't. Only this age. Only flat on his back, arms outstretched, smiling, swirling.

"Quiet."

"Did you know?"

"No."

What was there to know? Who can point to a day, a year, and say, this is when he was lost to us?

I sit and press my spine against the couch's swollen lip. The straggling crew left over. Misha, asleep against the far wall, bundled up in a windbreaker that'll soak through in a city block in this weather. I wonder for how long he and Elijah were lovers before Elijah faded away, like he did with all of them.

Kendra says, "When did you hear from him last?"

The guy hesitates. His friend sitting across from Kendra says, "There was a package."

In the corner, Misha lifts his head. "What was in it?"

"Books."

"Books?"

"Just lots of"—he looks embarrassed, as if by Elijah's tacky taste—"lots of self-help books."

My laugh, an ugly fish slopping from my mouth. Twelve Steps To Happiness; The Decluttered Mind; Change Your Life Today. The guy looks at me questioningly, and I am surprised by tears that suddenly fill his eyes, burst from underneath his rings of dark blue, and fall over his cheeks. Elijah was away for years, but maybe that's nothing if you're from the same tiny place. I look back at him and wonder again why none of Elijah's siblings are here. I think, I could give you some answers, some relief. That Elijah began collecting those books after he really started to lose it. That he read those books scrupulously and highlighted passages and emailed me the catalogues of his minor epiphanies, which often metastasized into groaning organs of Gmail chains. Sometimes I woke to thirty, forty new emails from Elijah. He probably sent that box of books to you and forgot afterwards. It could all mean nothing, so don't look too closely. I don't say this. I give Elijah the final word. He mailed that town a disco ball in a garbage can—*thanks for nothing, I raise you everything.*

Long

When he starts to run, he can't stop. He planned it as an overnight thing, a break. *I needed a break,* he tells me. The distances around his town can't be measured by the eye. Shades, green and brown, stretching over rivers and sky-line. He has never travelled over long distances without a truck, a long line of cars full of people like him. After a few hours, his feet ache. One of his toes feels like it's broken. He stops, takes off his socks and shoes, and keeps going. They all wear the same cheap shoes, all the kids. Black and square-ish. Fucking hideous, he tells me. His whole life, he's felt like he's in drag, in that white and black and grey world. When he starts to remember, in university, those are the colours that his weeks running arrive in. Black trees, grey fields, water flowing white. The smoke drifts around us as he goes on. He knows they're searching for him. He sees his face on a TV in a diner, through the window. He rushes in, uses the washroom, rushes out again, and keeps going. He's fifteen, he can't do whatever he wants. He's ready. In a fucked-up way, they prepared him for this. The alone-ness, the sheer stamina of continuing on his aching feet, of doubling down on all his pain. He knows to stay away from highways. He follows fences instead. If you want to find your way, he tells me, walk under a power line. The power lines take him down a vast path along the side of a mountain. He jogs and walks slowly, taking his time, because there's always the chance that when he gets to where he's going, they'll find him, send him back. He will wait until he's eighteen to send a letter, to tell them he's still here. For now, he's a boy walking under twin wires guiding him across the sky, summoned forward by their charge, arms channelling signals, a body telegraphed into the future.

Change Your Life Today

THERE IS A GAME SOMA LIKES TO PLAY.

When Soma closes her eyes, the classroom stops. When she opens her eyes, everything has slipped a little forward. She closes her eyes and opens them, testing the slippage. A game she's taught herself: she counts the number of things that change in the interval. Elbows in afternoon migrations across portions of desks, black lines on the clock, a person passing in the hallway. Increments, tiny markings only she pays attention to. Sundial of darkening elbow. Rain floods the fields outside the row of scratched windows and the crows and seagulls arrive by the hundreds, whole shimmering islands of polished feathers, an ocean of joyous cries. The sound crashes against the ash-grey stucco walls of the school. The water level rises to the edges of the windows and the birds beat it back down. A man in an orange uniform mows the grass on his machine. He rides steadily into the water until the birds surround him and lift him toward the sky. Soma watches him leave this world. Some kid told her that the school was built on a swamp, and if there's ever an earthquake, the school will sink—just sink right into the ground and be covered by water. *Water table*, the kid told Soma. *We're right on the water table here.* Soma pictured a

149

dinner table set with polished silver and plates, floating off on the Pacific. He said this like a threat. It always rains a lot here—steadily, for three or four months of the year—but this year it's bad, with flood warnings on the radio.

Soma closes her eyes, opens them. Her ears are growing in power day by day. Her ears are developing into dog ears, she thinks. Getting better at noticing the pauses, parsing the lifts. Every strand in the carpet scrapes her eardrum, a field of swaying grass.

In this way, she makes the hours in class go by, easily.

By lunchtime, the birds are always gone.

There is just the rain. Rain so complete it's not water, but resonance. A shallow lake dangles from the city's shores. Wheels and curbs. If the city were nudged slightly, it would hydroplane, skid away into the blue-white electric foam sky, but the rain would continue and new people would evolve, would naturally develop the ability to breathe underwater. These days Soma is watching her mother more closely than ever, since her mother went to her friends' place for a little more than three weeks, then came back, quiet. Her mother leaves, always comes back stronger. Using her dog powers, Soma can track invisible things. She can predict people's movement so precisely that sometimes, she is psychic. There's really no difference when you actually think about it.

In art period the teacher tells the class to copy down a map of the city and tapes a black-and-white grid to the wall. Soma tries for a while, then gives up when her streets come out all wrong, veer together like a fist of sticks. So instead she draws a big lake. It isn't a perfect circle, so she scribbles it out and traces a circle with the bottom of a pencil cup. Rain falls onto the surface of the lake, covering the buildings. Apartment buildings tower through the surface. A bunch of Starbuckses float on the water around the towers. Soma's mother hates Starbucks—*too crowded, the coffee's sour and a rip-off*. Soma draws herself on the roof of a tower. Scribbles herself out. Don't be silly. *Grow up*, her mother always tells her. *The faster you grow up, the better.* Soma will grow as quickly as possible. No!—no turrets. The underwater city has to be as realistic as possible. A bunch of tall apartment buildings. She draws people, a dozen, twenty people, all with breathing masks. What if someone loses their mask? Soma draws some bodies that have floated to the surface. They bump against the edges of the floating Starbucks islands. Nobody can just float around forever. Won't they get tired and sink, their sore bodies dragging them under, down and down and down? The classroom's windows bruise easily. Water palms the glass in many blues. The soccer field floods peacefully, reedy with western afternoon light.

This isn't the first time this has happened—her mother hasn't come out of her room for a bunch of days in a row. It looks dark in there. Sometimes a shadow crosses the line under the door. When her mother came back from the weeks at her friend's (*what friend?*), her father told Soma and her brother, "Mom is pretty tired, try not to step on her toes." After dinner, when her father is almost always still at work, Soma keeps the TV on until it runs infomercials for hours, letting a woman's voice reciting price lists tell her a story, put her to sleep. All over the underwater city, people are watching these glowing squares inside their apartments. Sometimes her mother comes out for tea, sometimes she doesn't come out until after Soma is in bed, sometimes she walks past the infomercials and says nothing. Soma knows never to knock, to glide her feet close to the floor. Her younger brother wavers around her like a shadow with translucent lungs, twin glass vases he carries carefully balanced on his palms, rests on the couch or reads in his room, on the evenings when he isn't at his friend Lucan's. When Lucan's mother drops her brother off, she never makes eye contact with Soma. Once, about a year ago, or maybe a few months ago, she said to Soma, "What's wrong with your mother?" Soma stared back at her, surprised that anybody had noticed anything out of the ordinary. She and her brother are the only ones who really know how things are.

Then, one night, while the TV is droning on, the infomercial for the light machine comes on.

A woman's face fills the screen, shadows covering a cheek and eye.

Are you feeling...
Depressed?
Hopeless?
Like there's no end in sight?

The woman's face rotates. There is bright blue light and she is swathed in it. The light source is revealed: a box, facing the woman with an irrepressible blue beam. The woman's hair flickers white and yellow. Her face goes limp, wrinkles brushed off. The voice begins again.

Soma watches the screen intently—her body has gone

stiff, her dog ears a bit numb. It's been raining, just raining, for weeks now. Her mother has hardly left the house. Yes— now she knows. Relief, a humming in the back of her head. That song they chanted in softball—*rain, rain, go away, come back again another day.*

The voice recites:
For when the weather lets you down.
Seasonal affective disorder has a cure.
Change your life today.

The woman sits under a cloud, separated out by the light machine, inside a zone of radiance. She is weightless, articulated by light. Every hair, every line in her face, every polished aspect of her eyes. Soma closes her eyes, opens them. Her mother sits in the space made by light. Her mother turns and turns, never glancing at the camera.

Soma's mother was supposed to be taking a break from work, but it's been months now. Nobody, not even Soma's father who works all the time, most nights and weekends, brings this up anymore. There's no point. Her mother will just get angry, want to know why they're picking on her. *Why does everyone always gang up on me?*

Twenty minutes later, the light-machine infomercial plays again and Soma copies the information down. It appears on the blue screen in flashing yellow print. 1-800-GET-LITE. Free delivery. Change your life today.

Voices circle from the bottom of the stairwell. Soma moves in the group of girls down the stairs. Fingers compete for the phone receiver, hopping on its silver tongue. Shea, a girl in her class who wears overalls every day without being teased, holds up a slip of paper and recites it again and again

153

for the fingers punching the buttons, a looped incantation of a 1-800 number. The group vibrates with giggles. From the periphery, Soma can't tell who they're calling—she watches their masks break into shock, seriousness, drawn mouths of something like pleasure, after ice cream or in strained sleep. Girls are a tide and Soma has no idea why she's here, at the bleach-and-sweat-smelling bottom of this stairwell in a back corner of the elementary school. The group of girls moved around her and somehow she followed them here, out of the lunchroom, and they're marshmallowed together in this underground corner. Every girl in her grade and the grade above is here. The older girls hold the receiver and pass it around. Mostly laughter and gasps, followed by a squeal. When the receiver is thrust toward Soma, she takes a step back. The receiver: black curved body with two faces, whining perforation, coiled wire hanging, and the sound coming from the top half. *Aren't you going to listen? What's wrong?* The receiver is cold on Soma's cheek. The sounds coming through are words, noises, not noises but words, extended strange breaths, a pile of sharp and soft sounds. When she opens her eyes, she sees the crowd of eyes mirroring her, appraising. She has no idea why she's listening to this woman moaning and sighing on the other end of the line, making sounds nothing to do with words. A growl, a sourceless want. She stares at Shea's face for clues to how to react. Where is this woman? In her home somewhere? In an office? Is she being held captive? She sounds pleased, and slow, and probably tired. Soma puts the receiver back to her ear and then it is grabbed away. A girl laughs at her.

My turn my turn my turn. Arms circle Soma from behind and she is turned, pushed out of the way, and for a moment she moves above the group and she is weightless, lifted, and then on the ground again, close to the stairs. The phone receiver levitates between hands. More girls arrive, a crowd of younger girls. They are pushed back up against the steps, protesting. *Get out, you'll get us in trouble.* Soma watches them go. A small girl with pale hair, dark eyes, looks back over her shoulder with longing and rage.

On the map of the underwater city, Soma draws cigarettes with boots and arms marching in a long line across the floor of the ocean. People mutter to each other, *cigarettes cigarettes cigarettes.* She draws big, wide smiles on some of them, furious triangle eyebrows on others. Her father comes into her room, says he will be gone for a week on business. He leaves.

In the place it has taken up in her mind, the light machine sits in the bottom corner inside its fence of orbital rays. Soma calls the 1-800 number she copied down from the infomercial to buy the light machine—the only thing that will help her mother, she knows. Ninety-nine dollars and ninety-nine cents, a voice recites. An unimaginable amount of money.

She hangs up. Her mother will always be like this.

The group of girls that comes to listen to the phone is always different, and so it's easy for Soma to take up permanent, floating residence. Always changing, the group has no memory. There is a tiny clutch of regulars, and always Shea, whose father's credit card is used for the calls. This isn't a problem because Shea's father is rich and never visits and rich people never look at their bills, Shea tells them breezily. They don't gather every day because that would be too obvious—a couple times a week the word gets around and it's always after school that they go, not lunchtime because there's more of a chance that a teacher might hear and come exploring the source of voices. Mostly they're quiet, passing the receiver around the huddle. The voice on the other end of the line does all the talking. All they have to do is say yes.

"Do you like this?" the woman asks Soma, and she says yes, like she knows what she's agreeing to. She has this feeling often, like she's agreeing to a deal she never intended to make.

It's always a woman's voice on the phone and at first Soma wonders why. Is there an option to choose between a male or female voice? Did Shea choose "female"? Shea is always the one who punches in the numbers and nobody asks her any questions.

Now there's a flood warning advisory out, and at school they are instructed in the basics—where to go to stock up on canned goods, to buy candles and lanterns and waterproof matches. Soma writes down everything the teacher says. She puts it in her pocket for safekeeping. There's a loudspeaker announcement—if a state of emergency is announced, they will receive calls to stay home from school. Soma prays, no, because then she'll have to stay home with her mother and her mother is getting quieter every day. Her dog ears are very strong now.

The field outside the classroom is completely flooded. Like at the beaches in the summer, crowds of people arrive and launch off into the water. Laura watches them. In sleek scuba-diving suits, the bodies are fast as fishes. They swarm the waters, hundreds of them, bodies under the blank, massive sky, a constant cloud cover that absorbs the days and the spaces between them. Soma grew up here, in this city on the coast, so sometimes she feels like a seal, or some other kind of animal who knows how to breathe underwater. From her desk, she watches the people swim for hours.

At home, she gives the list to her brother. He reads it, crumples it into a ball, throws it at her.

"This is stupid."

"What?" she shouts at him. "We need that."

He tells her, scorn in his wavering voice, "Lucan's mom told me if there's a flood I can stay with them."

"No you can't," Soma shrieks. "You're staying with me."

Her mother's door slams open and there she is, marks on her face from her pillow and sheets, hair sideways. "What's the yelling about?"

Soma's brother shrugs, drifts away, the way he always does—disappears into thin air.

"I didn't say anything," Soma mumbles.

Her mother scoops the list off the floor. She reads it over, a confused grimace. She laughs. "What's this for? The flood? The flood that's going to wash us all away?" She laughs. "If this city was going to go, it would go in an earthquake, not a flood."

Soma grabs for her list. Her mother moves it out of range of her small hand.

"So what?" Soma yells. "That's mine." Soma's brother is

at the door. This is the thing to never do with their mother—try to take something away from her.

"If there were a flood, you would go with your father and leave me alone here," their mother says.

Soma turns and follows her brother out of the room. He's running. So she runs too. His bedroom is too small for the three of them. Her brother is so small, wriggling under his quilt in the far corner of his lower bunk bed, trying to climb the wall into the top bunk bed, pressed between the wooden beam and the wall. Soma can't see him, just the movement and hard breathing of him, the quilt he's trying to hold up around his body. He's pressed against the wall, trying to fit through the narrow space. There's her mother, lunging, big hands filling Soma's vision. She's grabbing at him, trying to drag the quilt off his body. Soma jumps in between. She is huge—taller than her mother and ferocious.

"If you try to do that to him again, I'll kill you," she screams. "I'll kill you."

Her mother is gone. Door hinge, snap. Her brother shaking under his quilt, a bell in an empty building, but no sound comes out of him. Soma pulls the quilt off him, touches his squirming back. She looks down at her hand. She's still holding the list.

She's so good at her game now. She closes her eyes and opens them. Records the changes. She can predict almost everything. Which kid will shift impatiently in his seat, the arc of a yawn, a sloped arm travelling across a face. A few ants come out of a gap in the ceiling tiles and she traces their traffic down the wall, until they disappear. She closes her eyes, opens them. The room slips just a little forward. Not many people would notice the difference, but she does. When she opens her eyes, Shea is often watching. Her brother has been at Lucan's all week, so maybe he told Lucan's mom what happened with the list. But probably not—he's such a baby. Her mother has mostly stayed in her room, and she ordered a pizza three nights in a row, brought home Wendy's takeout in a huge paper bag, so things are better now.

Soma closes her eyes, opens them. Being with people is just an experiment in watching.

Every night in bed, Soma takes the map of the underwater city out of her pocket, unfolds it, smooths the crease that bisects the water world. The centre of the two folds places her mother in faint target crosshairs. Soma doodles a water-borne grocery store, full of stacked tomatoes in perfect, tight pyramids. She draws a tunnel from her mother to the grocery store. She fills the tunnel with tomatoes. She draws a couch in their house. She draws herself, chubby with shoulder-length hair and giraffe eyelashes, wearing her raincoat and a mask for breathing like a soldier in a movie. Under the city there are huge tunnels.

Two horses with long webbed tails sail past Soma's bedroom window, lights strapped to their great heads, starlight dispersed by their manes spirals in long spokes in their wake. They head for the surface.

Today, at the bottom of the stairwell, there is only Shea waiting.

"Hi," Soma says, toes touching down on concrete. Shea takes the receiver off the hook, holds it limp-wristed, casually.

"Is it only you?" Shea says.

Soma shrugs. "I guess. We gonna call?" Shea shrugs. Soma mimes Shea's blank stare.

"I mean, I guess. Sure." Shea slips the credit card out of the zipped side pocket on her backpack and punches in the numbers while she listens to the instructions, a seemingly endless series of digits. Shea holds the phone receiver to her ear, then shrugs at Soma. "We might as well listen together," she says.

Soma moves forward, and Shea presses the volume button. Laughter bubbles out of both of them as a moan spills from the receiver, the woman throws herself onto the floor.

"Oooooooohhhhhhhhhhhh. What do you want me to do now?" The voice on the other end of the line never waits for answers.

Shea whispers, "There are two of us now." Soma steps sideways and bumps into Shea slightly and, as she does, she dips her middle and index fingers into Shea's back pocket, grips the credit card firmly, pulls it out in one quick gesture, and slips it into her pocket, then sighs dramatically, "Oh yeeaaaaaaaaaaah uggghhhhhhh," while Shea bends, tries not to laugh.

Months later, when one of the other girls rats the group out to her mom, Soma will hear her dad shout into the phone, "Didn't anyone at this goddamn porn company notice they were talking to goddamn *children*?" No, the numbers from the credit card are the password to a parallel realm, a realm in which, when she opens her eyes, the people begin to move, and when she closes her eyes, they stop. Now that Soma has crossed, she knows she won't be back.

Sitting on the edge of her bed, holding Shea's father's credit card, Soma dials the 1-800 number for the light machine. Not a woman, but a silken male robot voice intones: *Thank you for contacting our purchasing centre. Someone will be with you soon to assist you with your request.* Piano music segues into a litany of solutions: hair-growth cream, knives that never need to be sharpened, a fish tank that cleans itself. Soma feels a stirring of doubt in her belly. These things sound cheap, not quite right. Her mother's word—*tacky.* Then the piano music jolts silent, there's a tone like an elevator opening, and a voice squeaks, with a thick accent, "How can I help you?"

"Hi. I'd like to buy the machine, that machine for—for light?"

"Pardon me?"

"The lamp. The big lamp."

Rustling. "Can you give me the full product name, please?"

"Um. The machine for people who can't deal with things without the sun?"

"The seasonal affective disorder treatment lamp. SAD lamp."

"I, um, I have a credit card."

"What's your age?"

"I am twenty-three years old."

A long pause. Breaths piped in, like the worker is an astronaut sitting on a picnic chair on Neptune.

"Visa, MasterCard, or American Express?"

Frantically, Soma examines the card. "Visa." She says her home address. She doesn't know what she'll do when the machine arrives, but there is no other address to give. It's the only address she knows by heart, the only address she has ever memorized.

At the end, she says thank you, goodbye, and when she puts the phone down, she is full of dizziness, a swampy buzz and shimmering through her, that she has done something solid, something good, something she can hold to her chest.

A secret: sometimes, lately, she leaves the house and goes for long walks at night on her own.

Walking, she closes her eyes. A man drifts at an alley's mouth. Soma opens her eyes. The man is gone. The alley took him in. It isn't raining tonight. The water level on her map is dropping. People bob. People swim to the surface on clear days and sun their skins, they flap their arms like ducks, they preen and compare their fins in the gusts of fresh yellow air. A bus swims past her, groans its air brakes, its myopic whale eyes move through her and away, into the swift current of the street. The gutters spit water and pulpy light. Fish dagger the corners of her eyes. She shuts them. Her lungs are bags of fluorescence that bulge when her feet hit the pavement. She is only light and water, emptying, spreading. Through the shutters of her eyes, she sees the people on the sidewalk lift, she watches their fins unfurl, and she keeps her eyes open as they soar above her toward the surface of the city.

The crows anchor the wires, bearing down the weight

of the city, its lopsided net, and she staggers forward and then runs, feet picking out the lines, darting away from the patterns, *step on a crack and break your mother's back.* Kids chanted that, they hopped and jumped forward and sometimes they fell and then they all went home. *Step on a crack step on a crack and you'll break your mother's back.*

She can see them, streaming from the rooftops and windows, all the people in fins. They bend their knees and launch. Their bodies heave upward on the tide, move gently with breaststrokes and small kicks across the arched roof of the street. Each one has a headlamp. They move their arms together, spreading out like a school of fish in luminous synchrony.

It starts to rain. The air rubs its glands against her cheeks.

Shea is waiting for her by the phone with a group of girls. When she took the credit card, Soma didn't think through how this would mean an interruption in the phone calls in the stairwell. Then, when she realized, she couldn't not show up to the phone—that would be a dead giveaway that she was the one who took the card.

"Where is it?"

"I don't know what you mean."

"You were the only one there."

"I don't know what—"

She's sweating under the bathing suit she wears under her clothes every day now. The bathing suit's material makes her feel lightweight, slippery. Right now, at this moment, she's hot and the bathing suit feels rigid, a suit of armour fused with her skin.

"I am going to have you *arrested*. For *stealing*."

Shea's tone is so imperious, so powerful, that Soma expects police to storm the stairwell, force her down in their black uniforms.

The credit card is in the top right-hand drawer of her desk at home, the map of the underwater city folded around it.

"You stole it."

"What?" Shea takes a step forward.

"You stole it first. From your father." Soma is surprised by her own voice – so loud, so even. *I'll kill you*, she had screamed at her mother.

The circle of girl faces behind Shea goes black. Then a couple girls nod.

"That's none of your business."

"Whatever," Soma says majestically.

"You can't come here anymore."

The thought of not being able to come to listen to the woman on the other end of the line is a small hard axe on the small hollow at the base of her belly. Lately, she has been wondering where she would go if she left home. How do people disappear? Where do people go? But she could never leave her brother.

"You can't even call her anymore without the card."

Shea, throat unlocked: "If you don't know what I'm talking about, how did you know I was talking about the card?" Her voice, without its restraint, is something desperate and grasping. Her face looks ugly, too.

Soma turns and runs. Behind her, sounds of a stampede. High breaths like birds screaming in their sleep.

Her face where a scarlet bruise will boom, against the cold floor. Her arms wrenched behind her back and her skin slipping off—no, just her shirt. Wetness on her arm.

A feeling like a tongue, but rougher, a mild scraping. She struggles to free herself and cannot. Her mother's face rages in her mind. Panting, freed, she curls into herself.

Everyone is gone. The fluorescent light examines her arm. A tattoo, permanent marker, the smell antiseptic, a fish-tank smell. Written on the inside of her forearm: PROPERTY OF SHEA. It will take weeks to fade.

Another rush of feet, and she slips her arm under her bare belly. Male voices. She's outside the gym.

A man's voice. "What in the hell? Oh my god. Stay back, boys."

In the school nurse's office, because she refuses to speak, she is placed in a back room the size of her kitchen cupboard at home. A nurse comes in and helps her swallow a paper cone of water. Asks what else she needs. Soma holds out her arm. The nurse returns with a length of bandage and winds it around the crooked black letters. "Shea did this?" she asks. Soma rolls away from her, wipes the two sides of her face on the wall. The bandage has taken away the burning on her skin. She hears the nurse leave. Who is she, another stranger, another open face, a window, or a just-bloomed flower, blank and passing?

Her father meets with the nurse and an older teacher Soma has never met before, a man with white hair and an old purple sweater. Soma watches them talk outside, a small circle of people, through the window.

In the car, her father drives a block, then pulls over.

"Soma, do you know anything about a package coming to our house?"

Soma shakes her head.

"A big box with something from the internet?"

Her light machine. It's here.

Where's Mom?"

"At Jenny's."

"Where's Josiah?"

"At his friend's."

"Lucan?"

"Yes."

"Is he coming back?"

Her father shakes his head, startled. "Yes."

"When?"

"Tomorrow."

"For how long?"

"What? He lives—he lives with us."

"Do you live with me?" Her ears are ringing.

"Yes." He sighs.

"Is Mom coming back?"

"Yes."

"When?"

"Next week."

"For sure?"

"Yes." Her father turns the heat on in the car. "Yes." He stares at her carefully. "I'm going to be travelling less for a while."

Her father turns the key in the ignition, and they begin to move slowly through the downpour. Water surrounds them.

"That nurse said your body was covered with bruises."

"Yeah, well that's why they called you."

"The nurse said that the bruises were new and old."

In the silence that follows, Soma looks at her father, his hands on the wheel, the sinkholes in his cheeks, his eyes glassy.

What if her mother never came back? For a moment, she allows herself to relax into the relief of this thought. Through his window, she can see a diver, padding furiously upward toward the sky. The clouds are dark, heavy with swimmers.

When they get to the house, Soma runs inside ahead of her father and takes the box from the kitchen table. It's much heavier than she expected. Her father offers to help her carry it and she lurches away, barely makes it to her bed before it slides from her arms. She gouges the plastic tape with a pen until she can shred it off with her fingertips. The light machine is packed in styrofoam pellets that she digs frantically through until her fingertips hit something solid, plastic. She runs around turning off all the lights in her room and pulls the curtains down. Her room is dim and quiet. When she unplugs her normal lamp, her hands are slippery with sweat, and she wipes them on her pants.

She plugs in the light machine, hugs the white cube close to her body. *You are mine.* Its broad, white-grey face flashes, before a strange, blue light startles her eyes and moves through her. The world vanishes, burned away. She closes her eyes. Opens them.

Her eyes shine.

A Brief History of Eye Contact

IRIS

You know what this is and so do I. Saying this thick with
teenage flavour. Lyrics from softrock stations for broke-
back commuters. Before these words are something too
much or something expected. Public school battleship li-
noleum. Cubism of regulation issue windows, doors, windows. Breaks in the basketball practice massacre sounds
in the gym at the end of the hall. Double doors, cigarette
smoke in atmospheric rings. Hung in a young lung. In your
basement, TV pickles faces, computer speakers scream
tinny desire. Clothes off. Sitcom family kitchen manners,
stuffed baked potatoes with their jackets off, a pile of warm
stones in the centre of the table weighing soft pocket of
your stomach down. Pass her like you have things, large
elsewhere plans. DNA sketched in the light radial piping
around the pupils. Breath-hold walk into your own mouth-
warmed air. Jingle and music smash of boys and girls leaning into the chain-link fence and bus fare in your endless
daily pocket. The row of sun-held second-floor windows.
But you aren't a boy are you boy oh boy oh boy. Your hips
clobber quick turns. They recognize you by your shyness,

your visible teeth. You aim your eyes on the spot beyond the bend in the hallway, the spot above the other person's shoulder, the steady speck on the wall. You avoid eye contact like a dancer learning to spin. With little effort, you can be invisible. Where are you going so fast?

SCLERA, THE WHITE OF THE EYE

Shame is a kind of magical thinking, Everybody in this school knows what you are feeling, everybody in this building knows what you are wanting, there is a conspiracy in the water supply your fantasies circulate with wings and indexed search terms everybody has a mimeograph of your first encounter your last dream your most recent browser history your skin has a visible bruise of every social brushstroke, for years you are blank a drifting transparency, you are a fresh street of morning glory you are a body projected onto the sky rainblasted billboard outside the town where your relatives live your guardian angel stole the photograph from your wallet last night eye contact is a portal with no record of crossing your stories were smuggled in a backpack to the beach where your ancestors were burned your incorrect face is tattooed on the palm of everyone you have ever wanted to fuck everybody reading this holds a record of your body's pale humiliations this paragraph has stretchmarks is badly juiced muscles bowlegged but only when lying on your back knees apart but really none of it happened it was thinking flying down to earth. Until the day someone looks you in the eye.

CORNEA

This is the year you begin to pay attention to bodies. There is a body you fit against, horizon, but also road. A space you slip through. A short hard barrier you curl against. You turn sideways and fall through the spaces in the changing of the guard. There is an interior chamber, holding light, refracting motives and elbows. Is there a way to be selectively neutral? Eye contact is a stream of alternate running storylines. You look for it, in the rescuing mercies of taxi cabs, in slagheaps of discarded magazines, in city hymnals. Habitat drift. Charisma is punctuation between the middle lovers. You can't hold a storyline, refract friendships like light passing through your swelling bent prism lens. Someone tells you, "You don't have to act like that, I already saw last night's episode on HBO." Nights rearrange plot and margin. You grow a body to fit every pairing. You are part human chandelier, part drag A&E biography, you are a chorus of labouring RSS feeds, and when you lay your hands down on a naked chest it is skin graft on candle-hot MacBook. In the coastal monsoon winter you fall asleep every night watching the same characters, walk through the sets in your dreams. Someone tells you, "People are limited," but you aren't ready to believe yet. If you look too closely, you'll give yourself away. When she takes her hand out of you, that warm space there, like losing your first tooth.

PUPIL

Someone tells you, "Every time I think about all the fur-niture I lost to that breakup I just feel so *angry*." And you laugh. You are a small space that time pours through as you walk backwards slowly toward the ocean. Your friends are tables and chairs crabwalking the breastplate of the continent. University is over, temporarily, for some. This relationship is on credit and I prenup my favourite sushi place grown-up pillows with feathered career plans and "oh him he's leaving town soon so I can tell he's fucking to a deadline." Love is a reason to move to a different city. Slowly your city becomes a graveyard of glass towers. A friend looks directly into your eyes for two years, then clos-es his eyes permanently. You guard the tiny portholes you carry around, eyes heavy as goggles. Dailiness is a white clay bowl you fill with bus transfers, proof of movement. The furniture crabwalks back across the Rockies, takes a long time, splashes into the Pacific. Float on your back, star-ing at the moon with its daytime manicure, its regimen of stars. Waves lift and drop the bodies and plans and botched partnerships and the tables and chairs moan, "It wasn't supposed to be this way." You have learned to look at eyes and not be looked through. High heels scissor you, slay you plainly, you have outsmarted climaxes by making yourself identical to the weather. A season later, you have outsmart-ed nothing. You should have disappeared long ago. You si-phon the newness of faces through your long black straw, dark point in your contemplation where all light enters. You want to be more than a body changing hands.

RETINA

You say: I will change for you but instead you only change. Non-adaptive traits include: avatar reliance, radio silence, sentences that sit cross-legged under the sheets. Your eye has shed its sheer glistening jacket. Inside you there is a rough screen and a shuddering nerve coming to life, cascading words. Pacing is what you were learning, walking to this. A body walks through the screen, trailing tendrils. Last things bring back the first, boys and girls marched along the borders, song lyrics doing celestial matchwork, your fumbling paws, your snakeskin that peeled back from your face like a cap in spring rains, a city underwater struggling against its own drowning. When you meet your match two chameleons melt into each other. Are you out there or in here? Both and more. People are people are people. You hold my sentences in the dark. Look me in the eye.

Acknowledgements

Thank you to the journals and anthologies that published these pieces along the way in current and earlier versions: *Plenitude* (thank you, Andrea Routley), *Lemon Hound* (thank you, Sina Queyras), *Prairie Fire* (thank you, Andris Taskans), *Word and Colour* (thank you, Leah Mol), *Granta* (thank you, Madeleine Thien and Catherine Leroux and the UK editors), *The Rusty Toque* and the 2016 edition of *The Journey Prize Anthology*, with special thanks to Kathryn Mockler and *The Rusty Toque*, for nominating me for that award. Thank you to Adrienne Gruber for reading much of this work over the years and being such an encouraging, warm presence for my writing. Thank you to Madeleine Thien for encouraging me to expand an abandoned short story that then grew into the novella "Who You Start With Is Who You Finish With." Thank you to the many writers in and around Vancouver who have invited me to read my work, eaten with me, and listened to me complain about "the process" over the years I wrote this book, especially Leah Horlick, Amber Dawn, Amy Fung, Elee Kraljii Gardiner, and Lucas Crawford. Thank you to Jesse Marchard and Liz Cave for friendship. Thank you most to Lorraine Weir, with love, for years of care and shared imagination.

ALEX LESLIE was born and lives in Vancouver. She is the author of the short story collection *People Who Disappear* (2012), which was nominated for the 2013 Lambda Literary Award for Debut Fiction and a 2013 ReLit Award, as well as a collection of prose poems, *The things I heard about you* (2014), which was shortlisted for the 2014 Robert Kroestch Award for Innovative Poetry. Winner of the 2015 Dayne Ogilvie Prize for LGBTQ Emerging Writers, Alex's writing has been included in *The Journey Prize Anthology*, *The Best Canadian Poetry in English*, and a special issue of *Granta* spotlighting Canadian writing, co-edited by Madeleine Thien and Catherine Leroux.

Colophon

Distributed in Canada by the Literary Press Group:
www.lpg.ca

Distributed in the United States by Small Press Distribution:
www.spdbooks.org

Shop online at www.bookthug.ca

Designed by Malcolm Sutton
Edited for the press by Malcolm Sutton
Copy-edited by Stuart Ross

BOOK
PRODUCTION
WAR ECONOMY
STANDARD